The Warning

Even the book morphs!
Flip the pages
and check it out!

Look for other **ANIMORPHS**®
titles by K.A. Applegate:

the andalite chronicles

The Warning

K.A. Applegate

AN
APPLE
PAPERBACK

SCHOLASTIC INC.
New York Toronto London Auckland Sydney

Cover illustration by David B. Mattingly

ISBN 0-590-49430-9

12 11 10 9 8 7 6 5   8 9/9 0 1 2 3/0

Printed in the U.S.A.   40

First Scholastic printing, March 1998

For Alexander and Maxx Leach

And for Michael and Jake

CHAPTER 1

I typed "Bball24."

Then I typed in my code word, which is a series of letters and numbers.

I moved the mouse and placed the arrow on "Sign On." I clicked the mouse. And I waited while the modem dialed.

My name is Jake

Just Jake. I can't tell you my last name.

My name online is Bball24. At least, that's close to being my real online name. I have to be careful, even about that. See, nothing is safe from the Yeerks. I could give you my actual screen name and they could find me.

That would be the end of Jake and Bball24.

All my friends. And, just maybe, the entire human race.

You want to know what my screen name means? Well, I used to be really into basketball. I tried out for our team but didn't make the cut. But my best game ever I scored twenty-four points. So that's what Bball24 is about: basketball, twenty-four points.

Kind of dumb now, I guess. Basketball isn't all that important to me anymore. And not just because I didn't make the team. It's just that I'm playing a much more intense game now.

I'm an Animorph. It's a made-up word. You won't find it in any dictionary. My best friend Marco came up with it. It's short for "Animal Morpher."

It's what we are, thanks to an alien who died trying to save the people of Earth. He gave us the power to morph. To become any animal whose DNA we could absorb through touch. We use this power to fight the Yeerk invasion of Earth.

That's another word you won't find in the dictionary: Yeerk. But the word has a terribly real meaning. The Yeerks are a species of parasitic slug. Yeerks live in the brains of other species. They live inside Taxxons, inside Hork-Bajir, inside Gedds, and I guess inside a few Leerans. And, unfortunately for all the free races of the universe, they live inside the brain of one Andalite.

They live in the brains of humans, too. Human-Controllers. That's a human who isn't exactly human anymore. A human-Controller is a slave to the Yeerk in its head.

How many humans have the Yeerks infested? We don't know. Too many. My brother Tom is one of them. Marco's mother is one. Our assistant principal at school is one. We've seen human-Controller cops, human-Controller teachers, and even a TV star who wanted to become a human-Controller — weird as that may seem.

They are everywhere. They can be anyone.

And that's why we fight. That's why we undergo the nightmarish transformations into animal form again and again. Because our only weapons are the animals we become.

I connected at 38,400 bps. I wish I had a faster modem, but at least this one is better than my old 14,400.

Some offers popped up on the screen. Would I like to apply for a Web Access America Visa card? No. Would I like to buy a new antivirus program? No.

"You've got mail," the computer said with a sort of mechanical excitement. Like it cared that I had E-mail.

I clicked on the mail icon. Three E-mails. One was a chain letter. I dumped it. One was from some guy who must have thought I cared about politics. It was some stupid conspiracy theory. I dumped it, too.

The third was from "Cassie98." I opened it and read it.

"Jake, oooh baby, you are the man for me. I love your big manly shoulders. I love your piercing brown eyes. (They are brown, right?) But most of all, I love the macho, manly way you boss us all around, snapping out orders left and right. I think of you as the new Clint Eastwood. I must have you all to myself. Signed, Cassie. XXX."

I sighed. Marco, of course. Cassie seldom goes online, and never sends E-mail, and would certainly never send me such a stupid E-mail. Kind of a shame, actually. But this was definitely the work of Marco, using one of his many fake screen names.

I clicked on the "Create Mail" command. I thought for a moment, then typed.

"Cassie, you know I like you, too. But I have vowed not to get involved with any girl until my best friend, Marco, gets at least one girl to like him. And since we know that's never going to happen, I guess we'll never get together. Signed, Jake."

I sent the E-mail, feeling pretty pleased with myself. Marco would get a laugh out of it. Marco always looks for the humor in any situation and he doesn't mind if the joke is on him. As long as it's funny.

I was going to sign off because, as usual, I couldn't really think of much to do online. But then I had this weird urge. I don't know why. I clicked on the Internet icon and brought up the Web browser.

In the search space I typed the word "Yeerk."

I clicked on "Search Now."

It took a few seconds to get the answer back. I expected to get nothing. There was no reason for there to be a Web site using the keyword "Yeerk." Like I said, it's not a word in any dictionary.

But then, to my utter amazement, up popped the list of hits.

There was exactly one.

I clicked on the blue hypertext link.

And suddenly I realized we Animorphs were not as alone as we'd thought.

CHAPTER 2

"There's a Yeerk home page?" Marco asked incredulously. "What do they have there? JPEGs of Yeerk slugs? Links to other alien invaders' Web sites? Ads for Yahoo's alien parasites selection?"

I'd gotten everyone together. Not in any of our usual places, like Cassie's barn or the edge of the woods. I needed access to a computer. And Marco's was better than mine, so we all went over to his house.

Marco's dad works with computers, so Marco has all the latest, coolest stuff. At least by human standards. Ax was with us, in his disturbingly attractive human morph. Ax's real name is Aximili-Esgarrouth-Isthill. He's an Andalite, which means that his own body is a mix of

6

deer, human, and scorpion, with blue fur and a pair of extra eyes mounted on stalks.

"Why is it working so slowly? Lee. Slooooow-lee?" Ax asked.

I forgot to mention that in his own body Ax has no mouth. When he's in a human morph with a human mouth he finds it very entertaining to play with sounds. The rest of us find it very annoying, but hey, we each have our faults.

"Look, Space-boy, this is the fastest modem around, okay?" Marco said defensively. "Fifty-six thousand bits per second."

"Fifty-six *thousand*? Not millions, at least? Mill-yuns. Millie-yuns." He laughed. "I like that word. It makes nice sounds in my human mouth."

Rachel rolled her eyes. "Yeah. It's a swell sound. Sometimes I just lie in bed for six or seven hours doing nothing but saying 'million.'"

Ax was totally unfazed. "That is a sarcasm sound, right?"

"Sarcasm. Asm. Casm. Yeah, that was sarcasm, Ax," Rachel said. But she laughed in a nonsarcastic way and shook her head, causing her volumes of blond hair to shake silkily.

Rachel is my cousin, so I don't think of her as beautiful; but every other person does. She's not just beautiful; she's one of those people who always seems to have a special spotlight on them wherever they go.

But Rachel isn't about looks. I know this sounds corny, like something from a sword-and-sorcery game, but Rachel is a warrior. I don't know what she'd have become in her life if this war with the Yeerks hadn't happened. But once it did happen, it was like Rachel had found her place in the universe, you know? Like it was all some inevitable part of her destiny.

Personally, I don't feel that way. I'd be happy to go back to being a normal guy. But I don't know about Rachel. There's something fierce inside her.

"So, let's see this famous Web page," Tobias said. "I have to get home. There's some guy trying to move in on my meadow. I have to be there to keep up my claim."

"Another red-tail?" Cassie asked him.

Tobias jerked his head toward her. It was a very birdlike movement. "Yes. And he's tough."

The Tobias I was looking at was the same Tobias I'd first met with his head in a toilet and two bullies holding him upside down. But that was an illusion. Tobias had broken rule number one of morphing: Never stay more than two hours in a morph or you stay permanently.

Tobias is now a red-tailed hawk. He lives as a hawk, hunts as a hawk, and eats as a hawk. But he was able to recover his power to morph. He is

8

still a hawk. But he can morph into his old human body for two hours at a time.

If he stays longer, he's back to being human. But he'd lose his morphing powers forever. And he wants to stay in the fight.

Tobias has been changed more than any of us by all this. Not just physically. He's lost more. Given up more.

"Okay, here it is," I said as the Web page filled the monitor screen.

Cassie leaned over me to see better. She pressed her hand on my shoulder to support herself.

"This page is devoted to letting the world know about the Yeerk threat! This is not a joke. This is not the usual Internet nonsense. This is serious. This is deadly serious."

I looked over my shoulder at Cassie. "See? Yeerks. A Web page about Yeerks. Do you believe this?"

She shook her head. "No. It's bizarre."

The page had four icons. "Facts about Yeerks," "Suspected Human-Yeerks," "Types of Yeerks," and "Chat About Yeerks."

"Have you already checked all these out?" Tobias asked.

Before I could answer, Marco grabbed my shoulder. "You disabled your cookies, right?"

"His cookies?" Cassie asked. "Disabled cookies? Excuse me?"

Marco rolled his eyes. "You really need to think about joining up with *this* century, Cassie. A cookie is a Web browser tag that can give a Web site some information about you. Not *you*, you. But your screen name."

"I disabled it," I said, with a wink for Cassie.

"Disabled cookies," she said with a derisive snort. "Computer nerds have this ridiculous need to make up stupid terms for everything. All they want to do is make normal people feel . . ."

She went on about it for a while. Cassie believes in real things like people and animals. She's not exactly a big fan of technology.

"So. What did you look at, Jake?" Marco asked me, giving Cassie a disdainful, pitying look, which she ignored.

"Well, I looked at 'Types of Yeerks.' There's a drawing of something that looks kind of like a Hork-Bajir. But there are two other drawings that don't look like anything we've seen."

I clicked to that page. Up came the drawing of the Hork-Bajir.

"Not bad," Rachel said.

"Obviously, whoever drew that had a pretty good idea what a Hork-Bajir looked like," Marco said.

The other drawings appeared jerkily on the

screen. One looked like a standard, *Close Encounters of the Third Kind* type of alien. The other two looked like a Cardassian from *Deep Space Nine* and a Narn from *Babylon Five.*

"Someone's been watching too much TV," Marco said with a derisive laugh. "Ax, have you ever seen any real aliens that look like those?"

"Like that one, yes." He pointed at the fetal-looking *Close Encounters* alien. "It is similar to the mature phase of a species called Skrit Na. The Skrit, the immature phase, is like a giant cockroach. This could be a Na. Only Na usually walk on all fours like sensible creatures. Reatures. Cuh-reee-chers. My brother, Elfangor, once had some big adventure involving Skrit Na. But he never told me much about it. The other species are all unknown to me."

"So. What does this tell us?" I asked.

"The accurate Hork-Bajir picture could be a coincidence," Marco said, "or maybe it's a mix of real information and bogus information. Or maybe someone out there knows more about Yeerks and the various species they've conquered than Ax knows."

Cassie nodded her agreement. "A mix of truth and lies, or else a coincidence."

"A 'mix of truth and lies' is like the definition of the Internet," Rachel said. "Equal parts reality and delusion."

11

"It's the same thing in the 'Facts about Yeerks' and the section about human-Controllers. Not that they use the term 'Controllers,'" I said. "Some of it may be true. But most of it is bull. I mean, it's like supposedly every politician in the country is a Controller. If that were true, the Yeerks would have already won."

I clicked on the list anyway and the others all crowded in close to look over my shoulder.

"The President," Cassie read. "Yeah, right. And the Vice President. Speaker of the House. Chief Justice of the Supreme Court. Good grief."

"Hey, wait," Marco said. "John Tesh is listed. That I can believe. Snoop Dogg? I don't think so. The Spice Girls? They suck, but I don't know if they're Controllers."

"This is ridiculous," Rachel said. "This is a waste of time. Some typical Internet wacko picked the word 'Yeerk' out of thin air and decided to make a Web page. It doesn't mean anything."

"That was my reaction, too," I said. "Then I saw this name." I used the mouse to point.

"Chapman!" Rachel said. "Huh."

Chapman is our assistant principal. He's also a high-ranking Yeerk and a major supervisor of The Sharing. The Sharing is a front organization. They pretend to be a sort of coed Boy Scouts or whatever, but they are a Yeerk organization.

Which made me wonder. "So if whoever put this page together really knows anything about Yeerks, why isn't there anything about The Sharing?"

Cassie nodded. "Good question. Maybe they don't know about The Sharing."

"Or maybe this whole thing is nothing but a Yeerk trap," Tobias said.

"Exactly," Rachel agreed. "Then they wouldn't want anyone knowing what The Sharing really is, would they?"

"So why mention Chapman?"

"It's a pretty common name," Marco pointed out. "Could be random. Could be coincidence."

I pushed back from the computer and looked at my friends. "If this thing is real, then maybe we have allies out there who could help us."

"But if it's just a Yeerk trap then we could be the mice, and this stupid Web page could be the cheese," Rachel said.

We all just kind of looked at each other for a while, shrugging.

Then Cassie said, "What about the chat room?"

"There's supposedly a scheduled chat starting right about now," I said. "But I wasn't sure if it was safe for one of us to go there. A chat room goes beyond just disabling cookies. How secure are screen names?"

Marco grinned. "A lot more secure after I get done. See, I have the access codes for the system at my dad's work. So I can hack in through —"

"Excuse me, Prince Jake," Ax interrupted, "but if you would like I can encode Marco's software in a way that will make it impossible for anyone to trace you. Why is it called software?"

I glanced at Marco. He's proud of his skills. But the truth is, Ax is about three centuries ahead of us in computers.

Marco threw up his hands. "Fine. Go for it."

"There is only so much I can do with this very primitive system," Ax said. "Two-dimensional screen, an actual keyboard instead of a decent psychic link, rigid codes . . . I'm not an archaeologist. I don't know much about ancient types of computers."

Just the same, he sat down and in three minutes had typed in a code that made Marco's system hack-proof.

"Okay. So. Do we chat about Yeerks?" Cassie asked.

"Yep. We chat about Yeerks."

CHAPTER 3

If you've never seen a computer chat room before, it's kind of confusing. It's like a conversation between people who aren't really listening to each other.

Plus everyone can only type about ten words at a time, so it gets pretty confusing. But you get used to making sense of it after a while.

The six of us watched, fascinated, as the conversation went scrolling down the screen. A conversation about things we thought only we knew about.

```
YeerKiller9:    there's no way!
GoVikes:        You have to chop them
                up to be sure they're
                really
```

Chazz:	Why don't we get serious here? The Yeerks are
GoVikes:	dead.
YeerKiller9:	Listen to me, I was infested by a Yeerk. It
Chazz:	only getting stronger. And instead of using this Chat to plan
YrkH8er:	Kill all Yeerks!
Gump8293:	I think my dad is one. What can I do?
Chazz:	some action, we end up doing nothing.
YeerKiller9:	was only by a miracle I escaped.
Gump8293:	I mean it's weird because my dad actually seems in some ways. But
GoVikes:	Yeerks are like worms. If you just cut them in
CKDsweet:	can anyone help me? There's this organization called
GoVikes:	half they just grow again.
Gump8293:	he is too nice. He's

16

```
                    got all these new friends
                    suddenly and
YrkH8er:    Kill all Yeerks!
CKDsweet:   the sharing, and I think
                    they are all Yeerks.
```

I looked at Marco. He nodded.

"The Sharing," he muttered. "Interesting. See if anyone stomps on that."

Sure enough, someone did. The supposedly enthusiastic Yeerk hater.

```
YrkH8er:    The sharing is okay. I
                    checked them out.
Chazz:      Wrong. The sharing is a
                    Yeerk front organization.
YrkH8er:    No way. They're like Boy
                    Scouts.
```

"Whoa," Rachel said.

"This Chazz guy seems fairly serious," Tobias offered.

"YrkH8er may be a Controller himself," I said.

"Or he may just be mistaken," Cassie pointed out.

```
Gump8293:   he's with them all the
                    time. The other day I
```

Carlito:	I've discovered that Yeerks need to go some-place secret and
Gump8293:	heard my dad and these new friends whispering about
Carlito:	feed or replenish. Every three days. I think they
Gump8293:	someone called "Visher" or "Vister" or something.
Carlito:	get out of their host body to do this.
MegMom:	Gump, I think it's "Visser." I think a Visser is like a
GoVikes:	they're like snails, only without a shell.
MegMom:	general or something. I think Visser is a rank.
GoVikes:	Rank. LOL. Totally rank.

"GoVikes is just your standard chat room moron," Marco said. "But Chazz and Meg and Carlito seem like they may know something."

"Gump is sad," Cassie said. "Worried about his dad."

"Yeah, well, it's a sad world all around," Marco said harshly.

I had known for a while that Marco's mother

is a Controller. In fact, she's Visser One, a very high-ranking member of the Yeerk hierarchy. But the others had only learned recently. And Marco is allergic to pity so he has to act extra tough.

```
Gump8293:   Isn't there any way for
            me to get my dad to stop
            being
YrkH8er:    Kill all Yeerks!
Gump8293:   a Yeerk?
YrkH8er:    Talk to your dad. Tell
            him what you think.
Chazz:      NO Gump. Say NOTHING to
            your father. If you say
            anything you'll be next.
MegMom:     Gump, listen to Chazz.
            He's right. You can't do
Fitey777:   Hi everyone.
MegMom:     anything to save your fa-
            ther. All you can do is
            get hurt.
Fitey777:   I have a name to add to
            the list of known Yeerks.
Gump8293:   I have to DO something.
Fitey777:   Charles J. Sofor. He's
            the deputy police chief
            in
YrkH8er:    Kill all Yeerks!
Chazz:      Hello Fitey.
```

```
MegMom:     Good, Fitey's here.
Fitey777:   the capital. I am close
            to getting the location
GoVikes:    chop him up in little
            pieces.
Fitey777:   of a Yeerk feeding area.
```

"So, what do we think?" I asked the group.

Rachel sighed. "Who can tell? Maybe some of these guys are for real. But maybe it's all a Yeerk scam to lure people in."

"Like Gump," Cassie said. "They may be trying to get his name and address so they can warn his father, the Controller."

"I suspect a Yeerk scam," Tobias said.

"I'd go that way, too," Rachel said.

Cassie shook her head. "I'm not so sure. There's something real and genuine about some of these people. Not all. YrkH8er is probably a Controller. But Gump is real. I'd bet on it."

I learned to trust Cassie's instincts about people long ago. "I get the same feeling," I said. "Ax?"

"Who can tell? This primitive means of communication makes it impossible to judge. Now that humans have the telephone, why do they still use this primitive system?"

"Actually, the phone was invented first," I said. "This is more modern."

Ax laughed. "Humans. You invent the book first, then the computer. Puter. Telephone before computer. Very backward."

"Marco? What do you think?"

Marco tilted his head back and forth in a "who knows?" gesture. "If I had to guess, I'd say a little of both. Maybe this Web page was created by Yeerks to help them locate any humans who know about them. But at the same time, maybe it got a little out of their control. I mean, maybe Chazz, Carlito, Fitey, and Meg are all for real."

I nodded. "We need to try and find out who these people are. Ax? Can you hack in and penetrate the protected screen name files?"

I stood up and Ax sat stiffly in the chair. He placed his unfamiliar human fingers on the keys. "What is 'Caps Lock'?"

"Forget 'Caps Lock.'"

"Yes, Prince Jake."

I sighed. "I'm not a prince," I said for probably the millionth time.

Ax entered the computer's software and began to write furiously. But after a few minutes he was obviously frustrated.

"What?" Marco mocked. "A superior Andalite can't hack into the Web Access America computer?"

"Can you?" Ax asked him.

"No."

"Ah." He went back to typing furiously. Then he pushed the keyboard away, almost angrily. "The most basic systems are not usable."

"In other words, you can't do it?" I said.

"No. This machine and the central computer are both too primitive. I tried to reconfigure the software, but it is not enough." He brightened. "However, I fixed it so Marco will now be able to win any online computer game he plays."

"I already win every game," Marco lied.

"Your win and lose ratio is stored in the computer, Marco," Ax pointed out. "You do not win every game. You win forty-two percent of the time. Ratio. Horatio. Ray. Shee. Oh."

"It would be nice to know if these guys are for real," Cassie said. "We may have allies out there. And there may be people like Gump who we could help."

I held out my hands. "So? How do we get the real names behind the screen names?"

"If we busted into WAA's main office . . ." Marco began.

"Invade Web Access America?" Rachel said, grinning.

"Yeah," Marco said. "Invade Web Access America. Bust into their main computers. Get the screen names. And while we're at it, turn off that stupid program that keeps offering you a Web Access America Visa card."

CHAPTER 4

We Animorphs are like the world's greatest burglars. I mean, we don't steal stuff, of course. But when you can become any kind of animal, it's usually fairly easy to get into places.

Just one problem. Web Access America was not in our town. The headquarters of Web Access America was a couple of hundred miles away. Too far for us to get to. Even if we morphed into birds, we couldn't cover that much distance in the two-hour morph time. And if we stopped and demorphed and remorphed, we'd still never make it there and back in a day.

So we needed some other means of transportation. And that's why we were at the airport in the terminal that Saturday morning, watching through the floor-to-ceiling windows as flights took off.

"It's a one-hour-and-thirty-minute flight," Marco said. "Plenty of time."

"Right."

"All we have to do is morph, fly aboard the plane, try not to get swatted, and demorph when we get there," he said. "We can take United or Northwest."

It was just me and Marco at the window. The others were spread around the terminal. We try not to congregate together. We don't want to look like a group. Yeerk eyes are everywhere. They think we're a bunch of Andalites, not humans, but we have to be careful all the time.

"United or Northwest?" Marco asked.

I shrugged. "Flip a coin. Who cares? The problem I have is with the idea of being a fly on a plane. Lots of people looking to swat. And if anything goes wrong, how do we demorph on a plane?"

"You want to cancel out?"

I thought about it for a minute. Out on the runway, a 747 was rumbling down the tarmac, picking up speed for a takeoff. "Nah. I guess it'll be okay. It's a risk, but it's worth it."

Marco smiled. An actual, nonmocking smile, which is rare for him. "I remember back when you didn't want to have to make all the big decisions."

"I still don't want to make them," I said. "But someone has to, right?"

"Yep." He nodded.

"I just want to get back to a life someday where I don't have to make decisions that might get people killed."

"Do you?" Now Marco's smile was definitely of the mocking variety. "You really think someday we can all go back to being regular kids? You think after being the leader of the Animorphs you can go back to being Joe Average Student?"

"Yes, I do." I said it forcefully. I meant it.

"Uh-huh," Marco said dryly. "Come on, let's round up the others." He squinted to see the board announcing flight departures. "Let's catch the United flight. It leaves soonest. We have fifteen minutes. Gate nineteen."

"Is there a movie on the flight?" I asked, trying to catch Marco's casual tone.

"On a one-hour-and-thirty-minute flight? More like an in-flight cartoon."

We found the others, drifting from Cassie and Rachel to Tobias and Ax. We explained the plan. It was Tobias who asked the question I had overlooked.

"How are we going to find gate nineteen when we're in fly morph? How good are fly eyes?"

Tobias had never morphed a fly before. He'd just acquired the DNA earlier that morning.

"Pretty bad, actually," I admitted. "Compound eyes."

"The sense of smell is good, though," Marco said. "I mean, flies can sense poop or garbage from a long way off."

I looked at Marco. He looked at me.

"Oh, puh-leeze," Marco said. "Where would we find it? And what would we do with it? Hand it to the flight attendant at the gate? Tell him, 'Hang onto this for us. We'll be right back as flies'?"

A plane was disgorging passengers from a nearby gate. The people all looked tired and annoyed. Some smiled for the relatives and friends who were picking them up. But I guess it must have been a long flight, because some of the people had pressure marks on the sides of their faces. You know, like they'd been sleeping with their heads leaned against the windows of the plane.

Then there was the mother and father with their baby. The baby was squalling and squirming in its mother's arms.

They stopped just a few feet away.

"He needs to be changed," the mother said.

"Whose turn is it?" the father asked.

The mother handed the baby to him and he groaned. "Please let it just be number one."

"I don't think so," the mother said. "I think you're getting a full load."

I turned to Marco, Tobias, and Ax. "Okay, we need a volunteer for a very hazardous and disgusting mission. Someone has to get that diaper."

It turned out the volunteer was me. Ax couldn't even understand the basic concept. Which left three of us. We did rock, paper, scissors. Whoever didn't match the others was the volunteer.

Tobias and Marco took paper. I did rock.

I swear somehow or other they cheated.

Two minutes later I had an absolutely vile Huggies wrapped in a couple of paper towels.

"I don't suppose you want this," I said, offering it to Marco.

"What is it?" Ax wondered.

"A diaper," I said. "Baby poop."

"Diaper gravy," Marco said. "We're going to use the diaper gravy to guide our flight as flies."

"I don't understand."

I sighed. "This would be one of those things I really don't want to explain, Ax," I said. I carried the diaper toward gate nineteen. I stuffed it into a large, standing ashtray and returned to the others. "That should do it. Let's get back with Cassie and Rachel."

"See, now this is why we aren't Batman or Spiderman," Marco complained. "Spiderman never has to follow the trail of baby poop."

"Who is this spider man?" Ax asked.

CHAPTER 5

We went to a men's room to morph. Cassie and Rachel went to a ladies' room. I guess there are times when we Animorphs just can't work as a team.

"We could all fit together in the handicapped stall," Marco suggested.

"You're not supposed to do that," I said. "Let's just each get our own stall."

But that was easier said than done. There were a lot of flights coming and going. The men's room was busy. The best we could do was get two stalls.

"Oh, this doesn't look too weird," Tobias muttered as he and I entered a stall together.

"Wait a few seconds. Things will be quite a bit weirder," I told him.

We closed and latched the door. We stripped off our outer clothing and shoes and stuffed it all into a backpack we'd brought along. We set the bag behind the toilet. You can't morph street clothes or shoes, just something form-fitting. Like the bike shorts and T-shirt I was wearing. If we were lucky we'd get our clothes back later at the lost and found. If not . . . well, we lose a lot of clothing.

"Fly morph, huh?" Tobias whispered.

"Yep."

"Is it as gross as I think it will be?"

"No. It's much, much grosser."

Tobias made a face. Then he started morphing. But not into a fly. See, when you morph you can only do it from your natural shape. Strange as it may seem, Tobias's natural shape is now that of a red-tailed hawk.

So as I waited nervously, Tobias grew feathers and wings and talons and a beak. And in the next stall Ax grew a scorpion tail, two stalk eyes, and four hooved legs.

"Ready?" I whispered to Marco.

"Yeah. Let's do it. It's crowded in here."

I looked at Tobias. Funny how even I was used to the idea that the real Tobias was the Tobias

30

with the fierce gold-and-brown eyes and the beak designed to tear apart flesh.

"Ready?"

<Yeah. I'm as ready as I'll ever be.>

"You might like it," I said. "You should see how well flies fly."

<I fly better than anything else with wings already,> he said. <Okay. Let's get this over with.>

I closed my eyes and began to focus on the fly morph. The truth is, it made me feel better to have Tobias nervous. It distracted me from the fact that morphing a fly made me sick.

There may be something more disgusting than a fly, but I sure haven't become it yet.

The first change was that I began to shrink.

The steel walls of the bathroom stall seemed to rise up and up and up. They grew to be the size of skyscrapers. Graffiti that had been in inch-high letters was now big enough to fill a billboard.

When I looked down I got a real scare. It looked exactly as if I were falling into the toilet bowl. That toilet bowl got bigger and bigger and seemed to be sprouting up from the floor like it was a big mouth trying to swallow me whole.

I saw the toilet paper dispenser go zipping by. One minute it was below waist level, the next minute it took off, straight up. It was an odd thing to see.

The linoleum squares grew vast. The scraps of tissue on the floor became bedsheets. A piece of chewed gum became a big, pink boulder.

But shrinking was the easy part. The other changes were infinitely worse. For one thing, there's the fact that your nose and mouth sort of melt together and grow into this insanely long, hairy, sticky, spit-dribbling thing the books call "mouth parts."

<AAAAAHHHH! Jeez!> Tobias yelled in thought-speak.

His own beak had just sprouted into the long, spring-loaded, utterly nasty-looking mouth parts. It was not a pretty thing to watch.

Sprooot! Two big legs sort of burst out of my chest. You know how in the movie *Alien* the alien baby exploded out of that guy's chest? It was a little like that. Only instead of some fake-looking puppet, these were two long, black, jointed legs, each bristling with daggerlike hairs.

Morphing is never totally logical. It isn't a smooth transition. It's not like each part of you gets gradually more flylike. Things happen suddenly, and in unexpected sequences. I was still about a foot tall when the legs pushed out through my ribs. I still had human eyes and a mostly human body. Aside from the monstrous mouth parts.

"Hey, anyone in there?"

I heard the voice. And I heard the way the door of the stall rattled. But I couldn't answer. I didn't have a mouth.

<Someone's trying to get in!> Tobias said.

<I know!>

<What do we do?>

<Keep morphing. It's too late to back out now.>

"Hey, is anyone in there? I gotta go bad."

My hands had become the appendages of a fly. There were two hooked, talonlike claws and small, hairy pads that oozed a kind of glue. I could hear my internal organs going soft and squishy as entire things like a liver and spleen and kidneys were re-formed to make the infinitely more primitive guts of a fly.

My bones were weakening so that my still-mostly-human legs were getting wobbly, turning to overcooked spaghetti.

At this point I was about the size of a small dog. I had fly legs but no wings. I had human eyes and massive fly mouth parts. Tobias was a similar mess. And that's when the guy who had to go bad reached over the stall door and undid the lock.

The door opened. There wasn't anything I could do.

"Oh. Ohhh. OOHHH! Oh, No! NOOOO! NOOOOOO! AAAAAHHHH!"

The man stood there and stared.

I waved one dagger-haired, clawed leg at him.

"AAAAHHHHH! Help! Help! Help!"

The door slammed shut again.

<Quick! We better be flies before he brings help!>

"Help me! Police! Someone!"

I continued shrinking, and now I noticed my gossamer fly wings coming in, attached to big springlike muscles in my back.

"There are monsters in the toilets!"

<What's going on over there?> Marco demanded from the next stall over.

<We're busted,> I said. <Make it quick.>

My human eyes dimmed, then went dark. Seconds passed in total blindness as my compound fly eyes grew. Then, all at once, I saw a world of shattered images, like a thousand tiny television sets all tuned to a slightly different picture.

<By the way, Tobias, watch out for the fly instincts,> I warned.

In my weird field of vision I saw something black and blurry go zipping by. Another fly. Tobias?

<Tobias, is that you flying?>

Rumble, rumble, rumble, rumble, RUMBLE, RUMBLE.

Thunderous pounding vibrations distracted me. Many heavy feet were running toward me.

WHAM! The door of the stall opened. I felt the wind whoosh past overhead. It excited the hairs on my back. My antennae quivered madly.

Danger!

I pushed off with my six legs, turned on my fly wings, and blasted up off the dirty linoleum.

<We're airborne over here,> Marco reported.

"They were here, I'm telling you. Monsters! Like . . . like weird, mutated things!"

"Sir, just how many drinks did you have on your flight?"

<Tobias,> I called. <Are you okay? Tobias!>

There was no answer.

I zoomed crazily around, zipping past the Statue-of-Liberty-sized humans. My senses were picking up about a hundred interesting smells: rot, sweat, filth, garbage. All of which were fascinating to my fly brain.

But I still did not see Tobias.

CHAPTER 6

<Tobias! Where are you? The fly brain has you. Fight it!>

<Yo, Tobias,> Marco said. <Come on, get a grip. We don't have a lot of time.>

<Tobias! It's me, Aximili. Reassert your individual consciousness.>

<Say what?> Marco laughed. <Reassert his what?>

Then there came a shaky, uncertain thought-speak voice. <Uh, hello? It's me. I mean, it's me, Tobias.>

I was inscribing crazed fly circles around the bathroom. I did a quick somersault and landed upside down on the ceiling. My claws gripped tiny irregularities in the paint. And the sticky pads on my feet did the rest.

<Tobias? Where are you? Are you okay?>

<I guess I kind of lost it there for a minute.>

<Well, that happens sometimes with a new morph. You know, until you get used to the animal's instincts.>

<Yeah,> Marco said. <But then you can "reassert your individual consciousness.">

<Tobias, where are you?>

<Well . . . it's smooth. Um, it was different when I first landed here. It was smooth and white. Wet, though. There's dampness on the surface. And I think there's a big lake or something below me.>

<Are you right side up or what?>

<I'm sideways. I'm sideways on a smooth, damp surface I think was white. And there's a big lake below me.>

We all considered that description for a moment.

<Oh, man!> Marco yelled. <Tobias, you're in a toilet!>

<Tobias, get out of there before someone flushes,> I said, stifling the urge to laugh.

<Um . . . remember how I said it was different when I first landed here? It was light. Now it's dark.>

We all considered this new information for a moment.

<Uh, guh-ROSS!> Marco said, half-laughing, half-scared.

<Tobias, I think the reason it got dark is that someone sat down.>

<Wait. You're saying I'm in a toilet bowl. And someone sat down. But then . . . oh, man.>

<Caution: falling objects,> Marco said.

<What does all this mean?> Ax wondered.

<Tobias, I think for the sake of safety, and also for the sake of avoiding something way too gross to even think about, you need to get out of there.>

<How? How? The exit is blocked, to say the least!>

<Try the space between the toilet seat and the porcelain.>

<Oh.>

<Look for the light. There will be some light shining through,> I said.

<Go into the light,> Marco said.

<Get out of there!>

<The space! I found the space!>

<I am completely confused,> Ax confessed.

<Okay, I'm out,> Tobias said. <This so totally sucks. I'm starting to wish the Ellimist had never given me back my morphing powers.>

<It's the glamorous life of a superhero,> Marco said.

<Speaking of glamour, we need to find the gate and get on that plane,> I reminded everyone. <Rachel and Cassie are probably already there.>

<I can find the door from the air currents,> Tobias said.

<Yeah. Fly against the influx of air. That should get us out into the terminal. Then all we have to do is pick up the scent of that diaper and follow it to the gate.>

<Hey, Tobias can lead the way,> Marco said brightly. <He sort of has experience at that kind of thing.>

<Oh, shut up,> Tobias grumbled.

<Will you explain what has been going on?> Ax asked.

<When you get older maybe,> Marco said.

CHAPTER 7

I wasn't lying when I'd told Tobias that flying as a fly is cool. I mean, in some ways it's bad because you can't see very well, so you don't get to look around while you're flying.

But nothing flies like a fly. Compared to a fly, any bird is a big, lumbering, clumsy whale. Flies can fly straight up. Straight down. They can turn in less than the blink of an eye. And I'm talking a full, one-hundred-eighty-degree turn in midair, no problem. They can fly on their sides and upside down. They can do loops and figure eights. They can fly figure eights inside a small juice glass.

And unlike birds, flies can land on anything. Anything. Horizontal, vertical, rough, smooth, wet, dry, still or moving, living or not.

They are very amazing insects. Very gross, very amazing insects.

<Okay, this is cool,> Tobias said. <Once you get past the fact that your own body makes you want to throw up.>

<Marco feels that way in his human body,> Rachel said gleefully.

We had located Cassie and Rachel in the air near the dirty diaper.

<Oooh. Don't hurt me with the chakram of your wit, *Xena*,> Marco said.

<Huh?>

<Chakram,> Marco said, like any idiot should know the word. <It's the metal Frisbee thing Xena throws. What, are you people cultural morons?>

Marco loves to tease Rachel by calling her Xena: Warrior Princess. Which isn't a bad comparison, aside from the fact that Rachel doesn't wear a leather skirt.

Marco and Rachel have a strange sort of relationship. I haven't figured out whether they pretend they can't stand each other but secretly like and admire each other, or if they really just can't stand each other. I'm not good at understanding subtle human behavior. I kind of rely on Cassie for that.

<So what now?> Tobias asked.

<Now we get on the plane,> I said. <But look.

Everyone be very careful. Use those fly instincts: Something moves toward you, get out of the way.>

<I can more or less see the gate,> Cassie said. <No, wait, I think it may be the window. That's the problem: The gate doesn't have enough contrast between light and dark for us to see it clearly.>

<Get close to a person. Stay with that person till you're in the walkway. We can figure it out from there.>

I saw a human head below me. Zoomed down toward it. No! I pulled back. The guy was bald. He'd probably have felt me land. There! A woman with big hair. Excellent. I landed on hairs like starched anchor cables. I could feel the breeze blowing past as we moved slowly forward.

The quality of the light changed and the sounds I heard seemed to echo. We were in the access tunnel. Then, a voice saying, "Hello, welcome aboard!"

I was aboard the jet. <Everyone here?> I asked. They were. I breathed a sigh of relief. Actually, that's just an expression. I had no lungs.

I landed on the overhead. It was perforated plastic. Lots of holes in what looked like a circular pattern. I straddled one of the holes and looked down at the people getting into their seats.

<Ax, keep track of the time, okay?>

<Yes, Prince Jake.>

<You know I don't want you to call me Prince Jake. I am not a prince.>

<Yes, Prince Jake, I know.>

<Good, as long as we're clear on that.>

We waited. And we waited. And Ax counted off the minutes. Andalites have a natural ability to keep track of time. It had been fifteen minutes since we'd morphed in the men's room.

Finally, I felt the deep, disturbing vibrations from the engines go higher and higher. I realized I was resting on the cover for a speaker when the flight attendant announced everyone should put on seat belts. The sound nearly blew me off my perch.

I zipped around aimlessly for a minute before coming to rest on the latch of an overhead luggage rack.

<How's everyone doing?> I asked.

<Twenty minutes have elapsed,> Ax said.

<And how long is this flight, Marco?>

<An hour and thirty minutes. That leaves us fifteen minutes to get off the plane at the other end and demorph.>

<That's a bit tight,> Rachel observed.

<Yeah.>

There wasn't a lot to do as the plane rumbled down the runway and rose into the air. The flight was basically boring. Until they served the meal.

Oh, man, you have no idea how much my fly body wanted to go down and land on that Salisbury steak and splash around in the gravy.

But that would have been suicidal.

<You know, airline food tastes much better this way,> Marco said.

<WHAT?>

<Relax, it's a meal some guy already ate. I'm in the leftovers.>

<WHAT?>

"Excuse me, miss, but there seem to be a lot of flies on this plane."

I heard the voice and it was like the announcement that calls you to the principal's office. It scared me.

<Did everyone hear that?>

<Hear what?> Tobias asked. <Everyone's talking. The whole plane is — >

<Someone just complained about the flies. About *us*.>

"I'll see what I can do, sir," a second voice answered.

<They're going to see what they can do!>

"I'd appreciate that. See, I am on the board of directors of this airline, and I just saw a fly land in my Salisbury steak."

<Marco!>

"Yes, sir! I'll take care of it!"

<Ax! How much time till we land?>

<Ten minutes.>

<Okay. Everyone toward the back of the plane! Get out of first class!>

We took off, six suddenly active flies. We zoomed toward the back. We zoomed crazily along the ceiling. We zoomed through the curtain that separates first class from the normal people. I figured we were safe. Then . . .

Disturbance!

I felt the air roil as a huge object came flying toward me.

I stopped, turned, and shot away to my right just as five fingers the size of redwoods swept past, raising a tornado in their wake.

I landed on the overhead and tried to calm my nerves.

<Man, that was close,> I muttered. <Everyone still okay? How much time do we have, Ax?>

I never heard his answer. I felt a hand coming toward me again. I sprang off the ceiling, buzzed my wings, dodged . . . and was hit by the second hand. The one that had been waiting for me.

<Aaaahhhh!> The hand caught me! I was pressed back against a wall of flesh. It was like being swept along by a broom. I buzzed my wings, but then I realized one wing was damaged. I couldn't get away.

I saw the wall coming toward me. It was a thousand tiny images of doom in my compound eyes. And there was nothing I could do. It was one of those nightmares where you see something terrible about to happen, but you can't move or even cry out.

WHAAAM!

It hit. I felt the massive hand press violently down on me.

I had been swatted.

CHAPTER 8

I was in the crack of the hand's lifeline. And because of that tiny indentation, I had not died.

But I was shattered.

My left wing was gone, ripped away. My right wing barely moved. I was blind in my right eye.

Four of my legs were broken. But by far the worst was that my body, my green-black body, had burst open.

But there was no pain. No pain. Just terror.

<Aaaahhh! Aaaahhh! Aaaahhh!>

<Jake! What happened?> Cassie cried.

<Jake, what's the matter?>

<I . . . I got hit.>

<Are you okay?> Tobias asked.

<No. I'm busted up pretty bad. I can't fly. I

47

can't move. I'm like, stuck. Stuck to the ceiling.>

<Oh, my God,> Cassie gasped.

<He'll be okay if he demorphs,> Marco said.

<How is he going to demorph?> Tobias demanded. <He's squished on the ceiling. He demorphs, it'll be right in front of a whole planeload of people.>

"The captain has turned on the seat belt sign. We are beginning our descent."

<Guys . . . I feel like maybe I'm getting weak,> I said. <Woozy. My guts are all over the place. I think I may be dying.>

<Demorph!> Cassie yelled.

<He can't!> Marco said. <He'll be seen. There are probably Controllers on this plane!>

<I don't care. It's Jake. I'm not going to let him die!>

My mind started wandering at that point. Like I couldn't quite focus. I heard them arguing in my head. Voices . . . voices . . .

<Jake! Are you still with us?> someone demanded. I think maybe it was Tobias.

<Yeah. Uh-huh.>

<He is dying,> Cassie snapped. <Wait! I have an idea.>

Good old Cassie, I thought. *Good old Cassie. She was so pretty. She didn't think she was, but she was. Yeah. I remember back when I first met her . . . And Rachel was there. School? No, it was . . . it was . . .*

Suddenly, monsters all around me. I saw them loom over me, hover in the air, then land. They had huge, bulging eyes that kind of sparkled from all the tiny facets. They had hideous faces with these long, vile tubes coming out, like tongues that could suck. Their wings were gossamer.

They grabbed me with their clawed feet.

<Oh, poor Jake,> a voice cried desperately.

<Do we . . . do we scoop up the guts or what?>

<Just hurry!>

<Jake! Hang in there, man. Hang in there, man. Don't go away on us.>

<Jake, hold on. Hold on, we'll save you.>

And then a horrible jolt.

<Ahhh! Oh, man. The leg I was holding just came off!>

<I can't hold on! Too much turbulence from everyone's wings beating at once!>

<Don't you let him go! Don't let him go!>

I floated through the air. I was kind of serene now. Kind of peaceful. Although when I realized half my body was gone, I felt concern. But it was a faraway concern. Like I was worried about something I was watching on TV. Not something that was happening to me.

<Okay, okay. It's the bathroom. Jake! De-morph!>

<Come on, Jake, back to human now.>

What were they all yelling about? Yelling and yelling and bugging me.

<Jake, this is Cassie. Listen to me. You have to demorph. You have to do it now.>

Cassie. Oh, yeah. Her. I liked her.

<Jake, do it! Do it now! Right now! Become human.>

Human?

Sure. Why not?

<There he goes!>

I began to change. And as I began to change, I became stronger. I felt life flow back into me. A human being began to form, dictated by the patterns of my DNA. Submicroscopic codes, making a human being the way words made a book.

The world swirled around me. Hazy images became clearer. I was in a tiny room. A very tiny room. An airplane bathroom.

I caught my reflection in the mirror as a shattered fly face melted and surged and warped to become a human face.

<Are you okay?> Rachel asked anxiously.

I worked my jaw. "Yeah," I said. "I guess so."

There were flies in the bathroom with me. And you know what's weird? My first impulse was to swat them.

CHAPTER 9

Fortunately, no one seemed to notice that I hadn't been on the plane before I emerged from the bathroom. We were landing, so I guess the flight attendants were distracted.

Probably they noticed that I had no shoes and was dressed in a very odd fashion choice of bike pants and T-shirt. But, like I said, it was the end of the flight. They probably just wanted to land and go home.

We made it off the plane with about five minutes to spare. One shaken-up boy and five very impatient flies.

They morphed in the bathrooms. I sat on a black plastic chair and held my head in my hands and tried to stop my fingers from shaking.

After a while I noticed Cassie sitting down in the chair beside me. She didn't say anything. She just put her arm around me and hugged me as well as she could while sitting.

I closed my eyes and let her hug me. And after a while I felt my hands shake a little less. My insides were still queasy, like I might need to throw up. But I stopped shaking.

"That was bad," Cassie said.

"Oh, yeah. That was bad. But I'm okay. No big deal."

Cassie nodded and let me go. "Yeah, right. Jake, it's okay to be scared."

"No, no, I'm fine," I said. I stood up, but my knees almost gave way. I reached back for the armrest of the chair. And then I pushed myself up more slowly.

Rachel had gone to the Western Union office. We needed clothing and it turns out you can send money by wire and pick it up by supplying a code word. Rachel went to pick up the money and get us something approaching shoes at an airport shop. Now you know where our allowances go.

The others were just coming out of the men's room. It had taken them longer, since Tobias and Ax both had an extra morph to do to get human.

"You okay, man?" Marco asked me.

I put on a sheepish grin. "Better than I was,"

I said. "I like having my guts inside me, as opposed to having them smeared all over."

"Yeah, guts should not see daylight," Tobias agreed.

"Okay, that was exciting, but now we're here," I pointed out briskly. "We have a job to do. Let's get on with it. Marco? What's the plan?"

"We catch a bus from here to downtown. That's where the WAA Building is. We bust in, enter the computers, get the information we want, get back here, and catch a plane home."

"That's supposed to be the safe, easy part, taking the plane," Rachel said. "Let's hope the WAA offices aren't as dangerous as the stupid plane."

"Hey, we'll take a different airline home," Marco said. "We'll get one that likes and appreciates flies."

I tried to laugh, but I don't know if it sounded right. I hadn't thought yet about getting home.

I was sure of one thing, though. I didn't want to go as a fly.

We took the bus downtown. We got out, asked directions from a nun who, oddly enough, knew which was the Web Access America office. It was a few blocks away.

We stopped on the way at a Taco Bell. It was cheap enough for us to afford. And it kind of lightened my mood a little when Ax went nuts and started sucking up packets of hot sauce.

The manager kicked us out.

"You kids stay out of here. Buy your crazy friend a bottle of Tabasco if he needs it!"

"What is Tabasco? Tuh-bah-sco. Sco. Is it tasty and full of flavor?" Ax wondered as he headed on down the sidewalk, carrying our bags of tacos and burritos.

"Yeah, you'd probably like it," Rachel said.

The WAA Building was one of those medium-sized buildings, maybe twenty floors high and not all that modern. We loitered around outside, trying to figure out what to do next. And that's when a bus pulled up and a bunch of old people started climbing out.

Someone came out of the WAA Building with a big smile and shook the hand of the bus group's leader.

"You folks are right on time. If you're ready, we can begin the tour immediately."

We all looked at each other. "They have tours?" Tobias said.

"Guess so. I guess we might as well tag along."

We fell into step at the back of the group. None of the old people seemed to mind. Basically, I think kids are kind of invisible to old people unless they are their grandkids, or they're being rude.

We were polite and quiet, and no one said a thing.

"As you may already know, Web Access America is the largest online service in America, with over nine million subscribers," the guide said.

"Well, this was easy," Marco whispered to me.

"We're not anywhere yet," I pointed out.

"Now we'll start by showing you our 'command center.' This is where we monitor the ebb and flow of traffic across our entire system."

Marco grinned. "Like taking candy from a baby."

We traveled up elevators, and down a hallway decorated with portraits of guys who I guess were the owners of WAA. I only recognized one. The guide stopped by the oversized oil painting in the gold frame.

"And this is our founder, Joe Bob Fenestre. Later we'll show a short, entertaining film about the fascinating life of Mr. Fenestre."

Marco raised his hands and made a bowing motion, like he was saying prayers to Joe Bob Fenestre. Rachel yanked his shirt.

"Hey, the idea is *not* to attract attention, genius."

"I'm sorry," Marco said. He pretended to wipe away a tear. "This is Joe Bob Fenestre. I love Joe Bob. I admire Joe Bob. I want to *be* Joe Bob."

"I didn't know you were all that interested in computers," Cassie said. "I mean, I knew you liked playing around with them, but—"

Marco waved a hand dismissively. "It's not about computers. Who cares about computers?"

"Well, isn't that the big thing with Mr. Fenestre?"

Marco shook his head, like Cassie had said something insane, and walked away.

Cassie looked at me.

"Joe Bob Fenestre is the second wealthiest man in the world, Cassie," I said. "I think that's what Marco cares about more than computers. Hey, Marco?"

"What?"

"How much is Fenestre worth?"

"*Mr.* Fenestre is worth twenty-four point nine billion dollars. That's billion. What a 'b.' As in billion."

"Is that a lot of dollars?" Ax asked.

"You could buy all the Tabasco sauce in the world with it, Ax. All the Tabasco in the entire world, and have enough left over to buy your own small country."

We turned a corner, and there, through the glass, we saw the command center. It looked like ground control at NASA. Row after row of men and women sitting at computer consoles.

We dropped back from the tour group so we could talk privately.

"Okay, there it is," I said. "Now how do we get in?"

CHAPTER 10

"How *do* we get in?" Rachel asked. "It's daytime. There are people around. This isn't how we usually do things. It's usually night."

I glanced around. The tour group was moving off. Pretty soon someone would notice us hanging around. People were coming and going from the command center down below. But it was awfully hard to imagine what kind of animal morph we could use to sneak in there and work a computer keyboard without being noticed.

I was puzzled. And no one else seemed to have any brilliant suggestions, either. I looked at Marco. He shrugged. I looked at Rachel.

Rachel said, "We could create a distraction.

Set the place on fire, then when everyone runs . . ."

"Rachel, these are nice, normal, innocent people, not Controllers, as far as we know," I pointed out. "We can't go around terrifying and endangering normal people."

She nodded like she understood. I'm pretty sure she actually did.

Then it popped into my head. "That's the morph: nice, normal people."

"What?"

"We acquire DNA from some of the people who work here. We morph them and walk right in." As soon as the words were out of my mouth I thought, *Wow, there's something not really right about this.*

Cassie looked pained. "Wow, there's something not really right about that."

"I think it's brilliant," Marco said. "Possibly immoral, but brilliant."

"Humans *are* the animals that are native to this particular environment," Ax pointed out.

"We like to think of ourselves as more than animals," Rachel pointed out.

"Why?"

She shrugged. "I don't know. We just do. Or at least as the best animals around."

"The best?" Ax echoed. "How do you define *best*?"

"We alone of all the animals have the ability to create TV shows," Marco said. "Why are we yapping about this? What's the big deal? Ax's human morph is made up of bits of DNA from all of us. What's the difference?"

"We consented," Cassie said. "We gave permission."

"Who cares, as long as it works?" Rachel said.

"How are we different from Yeerks, then?" This came from a surprise source: Marco. Was he arguing both sides, or had he changed his mind?

"We aren't taking over their minds," Rachel said. "We'd simply be using their DNA. No different from any other animal."

Everyone looked at me. Like I was supposed to quickly decide a big moral issue in a hallway in two minutes. What was I supposed to do? We were in a war. What was the big deal about doing something that made us uncomfortable?

I shook my head. "The whole reason we're fighting is to keep people free," I said. "If we start violating that and using people's DNA without permission, we may not be as bad as the Yeerks. But we're heading down that same path. We have to find another way."

Cassie looked at me like she was proud of me, which just made me want to blush.

"So how do we do what we came here to do, oh fearless leader?" Rachel asked.

"We go with a distraction. But we don't start a fire or endanger anyone. We just give them something to look at that is so fascinating and weird and impossible to ignore that they won't be watching what happens behind them. Ax and Marco are the computer brains. They go in. Ax as human, and Marco as himself."

"So Marco won't be human?" Rachel asked quickly, then laughed at her own joke.

"That was a good one," Marco complimented her. "Fast, too."

"Thank you."

I took a deep breath. "Ax and Marco go inside. The rest of us put on a show that no one will be able to ignore, then we haul butt out of here."

CHAPTER 11

We ducked into a small janitor's closet to prepare. Ax and Marco quickly headed down the stairs and around to the entrance to the command center.

<Everyone ready?> I asked.

<Yes. But I just want to say this is totally undignified,> Rachel complained.

<Do you have your mop?>

<Yes, I have my mop,> she sneered.

<Cassie? You ready?>

<Yes. But we can't lose these shoes. We don't have any more money.>

We had tied the laces of our shoes together, and now we looped them over our necks. All but Tobias, of course. I would grab his later.

<Everyone ready?> I asked. They were. <Okay, let's go!>

<Just one slight problem, Jake,> Rachel pointed out. <Who's going to open the door of this closet?>

We had morphed. Rachel was now a monstrously huge grizzly bear standing up on her hind legs. She was between seven and eight feet tall, with claws like the teeth of an iron rake and shaggy, rough, brown fur.

I had gone into my tiger morph. We'd deliberately chosen big, frightening animals no one was likely to try and mess with. We wanted people to watch us, but not try and grab us.

Tobias had become himself once more. A red-tailed hawk.

And Cassie had become the most frightening animal of us all: a skunk.

But none of us had hands that could open the closet door.

<Rachel? Why don't you just open it?>

<Cool.> She drew back her upper body, swayed back on her feet, and then thrust forward, slamming one side-of-beef-sized shoulder into the door.

CRRRUNCH-SLAM!

<There. Now it's open.>

We trotted calmly out into the hall and crossed to the glass observation window that

63

looked down on the command center. We looked down at the WAA employees at their computer consoles.

<No one's watching us,> Tobias complained. He was sitting on Rachel's head. <They haven't noticed us.>

<I can take care of that,> I said.

A tiger's roar can be heard for miles. Literally. Up close and personal, it is a sound you never want to hear unless there are some big, thick steel bars separating you from the tiger.

It is loud. And it's loud in a way that punches every button in a human being's instincts. I've seen that roar make brave men fall down. It turns their knees to Jell-O.

I sucked in a deep breath, and I cut loose.

RRRROOOOOAAAAARRRR!

<*Now* they've noticed us,> Tobias said.

Fifty or sixty sets of eyes had swiveled at once to stare up at us. And what they saw kept them watching. Rachel, huge, terrifying, powerful Rachel, was calmly mopping the floor, swinging the mop back and forth like a professional.

I was helping. I had the mop bucket in my teeth.

Tobias fluttered around us in a circle, shrieking madly.

TSEEEER! TSEEEER! TSEEEER!

Absolutely no one noticed when Marco and Ax

entered the back of the command center and calmly sat down at a computer console. No need even for a code word to get access. The machine had been left on by the person who'd been operating it. That person was staring up at us, eyes wide, mouth even wider.

With my acute tiger's hearing I could hear through the glass.

"Is that a bear?"

"Yeah."

"Is it mopping the floor?"

"Uh-huh."

"Have we gone nuts?"

"I'm not nuts. It's the bear who's nuts. That's carpeted up there."

"Why does it have sneakers around its neck?"

A few people screamed. A few ran. Most just stared as we cavorted around, having a fine time.

<Marco winked,> Tobias reported. <They must be doing okay.>

<Two more minutes, then we get out of here before someone down there thinks to call in security,> I said.

<Too late,> Cassie reported. <Here they come! Two guys with handguns.>

<Oh, man. Okay. We'll try and scare them off first.>

Two men in gray uniforms came racing around the corner into view. They had guns drawn. They didn't even notice Cassie, they just stared in horror and confusion at the lunatic scene of a hawk, a bear, and a tiger, all seemingly involved in mopping a carpeted floor.

I set the bucket down.

RRRRROOOOOAAAAARRRR!

One of the men dropped his gun, turned around, and ran. "Ya-ah-ah-ah!"

The other one was shaking, but he held on.

"Y-y-you animals g-get out of here. You're not a-a-a-authorized to be here!"

<You have to admire the guy,> Rachel said. <He must know that little popgun wouldn't stop either of us for a minute.>

<Yeah, well, it would stop *me*,> Tobias said darkly. <I'm just a birdie.>

"D-d-don't make me shoot!"

<Okay, Cassie,> I said. <I hate to do it, but take him out before he decides to shoot.>

Cassie turned her back to the guard. She raised her black-and-white tail. She turned her cute little face to look back over her shoulder. Then she dropped the tip of her tail.

If you ever see a skunk go through that sequence, leave. Leave, go far away, don't look back. The guard didn't know that.

<Fire,> I told Cassie.

She fired.

The guard, who had stood up to a grizzly bear

and a tiger, either of which could have turned him into raw hamburger, had had enough. No one, but no one, can be brave when he's been hosed by a skunk.

"Aaaaarrrggghhh!" He dropped the gun and ran.

<Okay, now let's bail!> I said.

<That was kind of fun,> Rachel said.

We ran, dragging our cheap tennis shoes along. We spotted an elevator. Tobias flew over and punched the button with his beak. People looked out of doorways at us. We roared and they went back inside.

The elevator door slid open. There was an executive and a bike messenger on it. They decided to get off when we crowded into the elevator.

Rachel jabbed a claw at the button for the lobby. And by the time we got there, the only people on the elevator were four kids wearing tight clothes and cheap shoes.

Heavily armed city cops dressed in SWAT team black were marching into the lobby carrying automatic weapons. Marco and Ax were already standing in a corner, acting like fascinated observers.

"Did you kids see a bear?" one cop asked.

"Yeah, right." Rachel laughed. "A bear."

We hooked up with Marco and Ax and went outside. I breathed a sigh of relief. "How'd it go?"

"We had no difficulties, Prince Jake," Ax said.

"Yeah. No problem," Marco said. But he looked concerned. Maybe a little sick.

"So, what's the matter?"

He shrugged. "No biggie. Once we got into the system it was a breeze. We had plenty of time. So I figured why not check out one or two extra screen names."

"Not exactly the reason we were there," Tobias said.

"This girl whose screen name is PrtyGirl802. She like sends me these very flirty kind of E-mails and IM messages. You know. Like she likes me and all."

"So you found out who she is?" Cassie asked. "That's not very nice."

"Yeah, no kidding it wasn't nice. I found out my online girlfriend PrtyGirl802 is actually a seventy-three-year-old retired postal worker."

CHAPTER 12

We had to memorize the list of names we'd gotten. There was no way to carry them. For the most part the names meant nothing to us. They were just names. And I'll only use the first names.

Except for the one name that really stuck out.

Joe Bob Fenestre. "Fitey777" was, in reality, the billionaire owner of Web Access America.

"No way," Marco said. "That guy hangs out in chat rooms? If I were him, I'd spend my day rolling around in big stacks of hundred-dollar bills, paying Michael Jordan to come over and teach me how to improve my three-point shot —"

"You have no three-point shot, Marco," I pointed out.

"— and having the female cast members of *Baywatch* apply suntan oil to my muscular body."

"So you'd have bought some muscles, too, huh?" Rachel said. "Didn't know you could do that."

"When you count your money in billions you can buy anything," Marco said. "Including happiness. Assuming that your idea of happiness involves a private jet, supermodels, and your own Papa John's pizza restaurant down in the basement."

"Be sure and leave your brain to science when you die, Marco," Rachel said. "After all, they're the ones with the microscopes it'd take to find it."

I laughed. Marco cocked an eyebrow at me, like I'd betrayed him.

I shrugged. "Sorry, but that round goes to Rachel."

We had taken the bus back to the airport. We were feeling pleased that we'd accomplished our mission. But I was worried about getting home. I did not want to go back aboard that plane in fly morph. But I didn't know how else to do it.

I was scared. Just that simple: I was scared.

But I was also scared of letting the others know I was scared. Weird, huh? Scared and scared of people thinking you're scared?

I was trembling by the time we got inside the

airport. I don't know if anyone noticed. I couldn't see myself trembling, I could only feel it. It was like when you have a fever and you get chills that make your stomach muscles shake violently and make you want to curl up in a ball and pile covers five feet high all over your body.

The others kept chattering away. And I kept adding a word here or a smile there. You know, so no one would think anything was wrong. But I was sweating. I used my sleeve to wipe my forehead and the sleeve came away as wet as if I'd dipped it into a sink.

"You know, maybe we should try some other morph on the way home," Cassie said nonchalantly.

Ah. So at least one person had noticed. Cassie. She was trying to give me a way out. Without embarrassing me.

"Why?" Ax asked.

"I don't know," Cassie said, with just a hint of tension in the way she kept her mouth tight. "It might be fun to do it a different way."

"We already went over it before," Rachel said reasonably. "We decided fly morph would work best, right? I mean, just because Jake had some trouble doesn't mean the idea is bad."

Deadlock. Cassie couldn't say anything more without it being obvious that she was trying to protect me. And I couldn't have that.

"Fly morph is fine," I said as coolly as I could. "Still the best way to do this."

I think Cassie was a little disgusted with me. "Hey, Jake," she said, fake-bright, "come buy me a pretzel. I'm hungry. You guys go on ahead."

Cassie grabbed my arm and hauled me aside. The others went on.

"That was subtle," I said. "I don't have any more money."

Cassie looked at me and shook her head. "What is the *matter* with you? You don't have to do this. You don't have to prove how tough you are."

"It's not a problem, Cassie. Thanks, but let it go, okay?"

"Jake, you may have the others fooled, but not me. You're scared. And you have good reason to be scared. So what's the big deal?"

I tried to walk away. But that felt wrong. I turned back to face her. "The big deal is I'm supposedly the leader of this little army."

"So? So you're not supposed to be human?"

"That's absolutely right. I'm not supposed to be human."

She laughed uncertainly, like she wasn't sure if I was joking or not. "No one expects you to be Superman, Jake. You think the others won't respect you if you admit you're terrified of something?"

"It's not about respect. It's not even about being scared. It's about letting fear tell you what to do."

"If it's unreasonable fear you have to get past it," Cassie said. "But there's a reason for this fear. You were nearly killed."

I shook my head. "No. You're usually right, Cassie, but this time you're wrong. See, if I give in to fear, then that gives everyone permission to give in to fear. And we all have good reasons to be afraid. Pretty soon we'd be totally paralyzed. We wouldn't be able to do anything because one of us might have some good reason to be scared."

"We don't morph ants anymore because they scared all of us, but mostly Marco," Cassie pointed out. "We don't ever talk about morphing termites because of my problems with them. What's the difference?"

"The difference is you all decided I was the leader," I said. "That's the difference. A leader may be just as weak or scared or doubtful as anyone else. But he isn't allowed to show it. People say they want leaders to be just like them, but I don't think so. People want leaders to act the way people wish they could act themselves. Marco and Rachel and Tobias and Ax don't *want* me to give them permission to be scared. They want me to help them to be brave."

Cassie looked at me a long time and I looked away, feeling uncomfortable.

"We didn't do you any favor when we made you leader, did we?" Cassie asked.

I forced a grim smile. "There's something else a leader doesn't do," I said. "Complain about being a leader."

"We did pick the right person, though," she said.

Once again I started to walk away, but Cassie grabbed my arm. "Look, maybe you're right. But I'll bet even great generals and presidents or whatever have friends they can be honest with. People who would never lose faith in them, no matter what."

I had the strangest desire to burst out crying right then. I also had a desire to hug Cassie really hard. I didn't do either.

"Come on," I said. "The others are waiting."

CHAPTER 13

We made it back home okay. No one swatted me and I felt better for getting past the fear. At least that's what I told myself. You never really get past the fear. Fear eats a little hole in you, like rust in the fender of a car. You fill the hole up with putty and sand it smooth and paint it over so no one else can see it. But it's never really as good as new.

I was exhausted by the time I made it home. My brother was in the kitchen, talking on the phone while he smeared peanut butter on a graham cracker. When he heard me come in he changed his tone of voice.

In the old days I would have assumed he'd

been talking to a girl. Now I assumed he'd been talking to some other Controller.

I unloaded a bunch of food from the refrigerator: leftover barbecued chicken and mashed potatoes. I plopped it all on a plate and stuck it in the microwave.

"I gotta go," Tom said into the phone. He hung up.

"What's up?" I asked him.

"Nada," he said, and left the room.

I took my food up to my room. I started to boot up my computer, but hesitated. Instead I sat down and munched indifferently while staring at the blank screen.

So. What did it mean that Joe Bob Fenestre was the so-called "Fitey777"? Judging by the chat we'd eavesdropped on, Fitey777 was a legitimate Yeerk-fighter. Not like the YrkH8er person who'd been an obvious Controller.

But it wasn't that simple. Joe Bob Fenestre had access to all WAA information. So he knew who all the other people in that chat room really were. He even knew who had established the Web page.

Fenestre had access to all kinds of information. He owned the biggest online service in the country. So maybe that's how he'd discovered the existence of the Yeerk invasion.

Or maybe the point was that the Yeerks had

seen how important Fenestre was and had made him a Controller. It would make sense.

Which left us no wiser than we had been going in. Was Fenestre a true enemy of the Yeerks? Or was he a Controller using the Web site as a lure to trap true enemies of the Yeerks?

We had to know. I should head over to Marco's house and get him to pull up any articles he could find on Joe Bob Fenestre's house. He didn't live too far away. He flew his own private jet to his WAA offices every day.

I was really tired. I felt like I could have slept for a week. But weekends were our good time. School days were tougher. And tomorrow, Sunday, was the end of the weekend.

I went downstairs. My parents had both just come in. They were carrying department store handle bags. They'd been shopping.

"Hey, Jake," my dad said.

"Honey, there are some more bags in the car," my mom said.

I brought in the bags.

"I'm taking off," I said.

My mom gave me a look. "Weren't you out all day?"

I shrugged. "I guess so."

"Would it kill you to have dinner with your family?"

"Is it dinnertime?"

"It will be as soon as I make that salmon I picked up yesterday," she said. "You loved it last time I made it. I mostly got it for you."

Guilt. Great. I smiled. "Well, you didn't tell me that's what you were making. Marco can wait. I'm there."

We try not to use the phone very much. Phone lines are too easy to tap. Plus I never know if Tom might be listening in. So I couldn't call Marco or Rachel. I'd have to do the research myself. If we were going to bust into Joe Bob Fenestre's massive home, we'd need some idea what we were dealing with.

I started on some homework while my mom cooked. Then my dad yelled up the stairs to say that Showtime was doing a rebroadcast of this fight that had been on pay-per-view. So I took my homework downstairs and worked on it with one eye on the TV.

Then we had dinner. The four of us. Like the old days.

My dad got off into some long, involved, really boring story about his work. And my mom asked me and Tom about school. Then my dad realized he'd forgotten some part of his boring story, so he had to tell that part over again. And my mom said she hoped we liked the clothes she'd bought at the mall. And of course Tom and I joked about how she'd probably shopped at Formerly Cool

Fashions "R" Us. It was an old joke we always used whenever my mom bought us clothing.

It was so normal. Tom and me. Our parents. My mom and dad squeezing each other's hands like they were on their first date.

I sat there afterward, stuffed with fish and rice and snap peas, and still stuffing my face with something called tiramisu, which is an Italian dessert soaked in some kind of liqueur.

I wanted to believe it was all real. Because, you know, that was the whole point of fighting. The whole point of taking risks and fighting the Yeerks was to protect boring, average, no-big-deal times like this.

I flashed back on being smeared across the ceiling of the plane. And I flashed on the time we'd almost been able to save Tom, down in the hell of the Yeerk pool. It made me mad. Mostly what people want is to be left alone. They just want to sit down and have a nice dinner and tell boring stories and tell jokes they've told a dozen times before.

But I guess there is always someone out there who thinks life, just plain old boring, sweet, everyday life, isn't enough. And that's when the killing starts. In this war it was the Yeerks. But there had been an awful lot of wars when it was just human against human.

What is the matter with people that they don't

know all that really counts is that people who love each other be able to be together, live in peace, learn, work, tell boring stories and dumb jokes? What do they think they're going to get that is better than that?

"You're awfully quiet, Jake," my mother said. "Thinking deep thoughts?"

I smiled. "I was thinking this was cool. We should all have dinner together more often." I looked at Tom. "It was nice. I hope nothing ever happens to us. I hope we'll always be together."

The Yeerk inside Tom's head searched Tom's memory. The Yeerk opened his memory and read it like a book. He played the strings of Tom's brain like a violinist squeezing perfect notes out of a violin.

The Yeerk found the answer that Tom would have made. It aimed Tom's eyes and made Tom's face smile sardonically. It opened Tom's mouth and made Tom say the words Tom would have said, if he'd been able.

"Hey, Mom, no more tiramisu for Jake. The liqueur is making him mushy."

I laughed the way I should. And I thought to myself, *The day will come, Yeerk, when I will tear you out of his head and destroy you for what you've done to my family.*

CHAPTER 14

While I spent the evening with my family, Marco had been busy. He'd used the hack-proof program Ax had written for him to go back to the chat room. He told us about it when we trudged out to the woods at the edge of Cassie's farm. Tobias and Ax could both be themselves out there.

"Most of the same people were there," Marco explained. "There were some new names, but GoVikes, YrkH8er, Chazz, CKDsweet, YeerKiller, Carlito, MegMom, and Gump8293 were all there. The Gump kid was still talking about his dad. I get the feeling maybe he's getting ready to confront his father."

"We can't let that happen," Cassie said.

"Gump is a nine-year-old kid," I reminded

everyone. "He lives close enough. Meg, Chazz, and CKDsweet are all from out of town. Some of them way out of town. That leaves us with GoVikes —"

"— an idiot," Rachel pointed out.

"— YrkH8er, Gump, Chazz and, of course, Fitey777," I finished.

<YrkH8er is a Controller, right?> Tobias asked. <I mean, that's what he acts like. Like a Controller trying to pass himself off as an enemy of Yeerks.>

Tobias was in a branch maybe ten feet over our heads. His talons sank deep into loose bark.

Cassie tilted her head back and forth like she wasn't too sure. "YrkH8er is someone named Edward Cheltingham. What was he? Thirty years old? But you know what? I looked in the phone book this morning and there was no Edward Cheltingham. Only two 'Cheltinghams' listed and they were both female."

"So? He has an unlisted phone number," Rachel said.

"Maybe so. Or maybe Edward Cheltingham is as phony a name as YrkH8er," Cassie said. "Isn't it possible to get a fake ID and a credit card in some name and then open a WAA account?"

Obviously, that had not occurred to anyone except Cassie.

"Oh," Rachel said. "Great. A new level of difficulty. So this guy could be anyone."

"We have an address for him," Cassie said. "We could check it out." She looked at me. "We also have an address for Gump."

"Gump isn't the point," Marco said. "Fenestre is the person at the middle of all this. He's the main man. Figure out what's happening with him, and you figure it all out."

"Maybe," Cassie conceded. "But he can wait. Gump may be in trouble right now."

"Look, Cassie," Marco said, "it's Sunday. If we go after Fenestre, it's probably going to take some time. Which means a weekend, which means today. We can check out Gump any day after school. Monday. Tuesday."

"Unless Monday is too late. Unless later today that scared little kid talks to his dad and his dad is a Controller, and that's it for Gump. Gump does a disappearing act. Or else ends up as the new home for some low-level Yeerk."

The two of them looked to me. I was supposed to decide which was our top priority. Rescue a nine-year-old, or maybe bust open the whole thing with a raid on Fenestre's mansion.

I looked down at the ground. "Marco, did you happen to do any research on Fenestre's house?"

"No. I thought you were doing it."

"I got kind of tied up. Big family thing."

"It's supposed to have massive security," Marco said. "Lots of computer stuff. But it shouldn't be any problem for us. I mean, security is designed to keep out humans, right? Not animals."

I nodded. I hoped he was right. I felt a twinge of worry, but Marco was right: Fenestre was at the center. "Cassie, first thing after school tomorrow, we'll check out Gump."

She nodded. But she looked bitter. "I hope that's soon enough."

"Yep. Me, too. Okay." I rubbed my hands together, shot Rachel a cocky wink, and put on my best "game face." "Let's do it, then. Let's go see how the superrich live."

I sensed I was making a mistake. But I didn't know what it was. And a leader has to lead, not sit around consulting his horoscope or taking his own pulse.

So I made the decision.

CHAPTER 15

You think you've seen big houses? You haven't seen anything till you've seen the home of Joe Bob Fenestre, WAA founder and megabillionaire.

From the air it looked like a junior college or something. Like a shopping center. There were a dozen separate buildings. Two guest houses, each twice the size of my home. A pool house with changing rooms and a bar that extended to the edge of the pool, which was itself in the shape of the WAA logo. A boathouse down on the riverfront with a sleek cigarette boat docked alongside. A stable big enough to house a dozen horses. What looked like an observatory. A greenhouse bursting with bright green lettuce and herbs and entire orange trees. A garage, easily big enough to store thirty or forty cars. A security building with armed guards next to a quarter-mile-long driveway. And finally, on a hill surrounded by a lawn you could have held the Superbowl on, was the house itself.

<This guy knows how to live,> Marco said with satisfaction. <Someday that'll be me.>

<Who'll be you? The guy mowing the lawn down there?> Rachel said.

<What do you think he's got in that garage?> Tobias wondered. <Ferraris? Porsches? Jaguars? Vipers?>

<Not minivans and Volvo station wagons,> Marco said. <That's for sure. Maybe a few Rolls-Royces.>

We were floating about a quarter mile above the Fenestre compound. Tobias was Tobias. Ax was in his northern harrier morph, Rachel was a bald eagle, Cassie and Marco were both ospreys. And I was in one of my favorite morphs: peregrine falcon. One of the fastest things alive. And with eyes that could see a flea on a dog from a hundred feet away.

I'd had a slightly bad feeling going into this mission. But I was feeling pretty good now. I usually feel pretty good when I'm flying.

When you are floating on a pillar of warm, upwelling air with your wings spread wide and no sound but the breeze in your feathers, you pretty much have to feel good. It is as free a feeling as you could ever imagine.

But at the same time I was noticing details with my laser-focus falcon's eyes: three separate fences. One around the perimeter of the entire compound, woods, gardens, pool, tennis courts, and all. Then a second fence about twenty yards inside the first fence. And finally, a third fence just around the house and its lawn.

<This guy is a little paranoid, isn't he?> Rachel said. <You guys see the little observation posts on the corners of the house? There are guys in there. Guys with guns.>

<And don't forget the Rottweilers,> Cassie pointed out. <Two teams of two dogs each patrolling between the outer fence and the second fence. Each team with an armed man.>

<Colonel Hogan would never get out of this place,> I said. I was pleased when Marco and Tobias laughed. <I guess now we know who watches *Hogan's Heroes* reruns on Nick.>

Cassie, with her osprey eyes that were designed to spot fish down below the water, said, <There's some sort of underwater fence, too. I can't see it all, but there's a definite line beneath the water.>

<Is this human in great danger?> Ax wondered.

<Nah, that's just the way rich people are,> Marco said.

<Okay, so how do we get into this place?> I asked. <Anyone have any brilliant ideas?>

<Fly right in through an open window,> Tobias suggested. <There's one on the back side of the house.>

<Then what?> Cassie asked. <We need to be able to move around inside the house. Find Mr. Fenestre's office maybe. And be able to overhear what's going on.>

<We could do flies again,> Marco suggested.

<We could do ants, too,> Cassie said, taking an uncharacteristic shot at Marco, who had sworn never to morph an ant again.

It was time for me to decide. <Okay, first of all, we go in like Tobias said. Only Tobias stays outside and uses his eyes and ears to report what he sees through the windows. Inside half of us morph to fly, the others to cockroach. We spread out and keep in touch by thought-speak. Anyone finds Fenestre, he calls the others. Okay?>

<Let's do it!> Rachel said as she spilled air from her wings and plummeted toward the open window.

Down she went, huge wings swept back, talons up, her blazing white eagle's head up to keep her eyes focused on the window.

Cassie was about twenty feet behind her, then

me, then Marco and Ax. Tobias caught an updraft and soared higher, up to a level where he could see everything happening on the estate.

Down Rachel went. Down I went, fast as a bullet.

Rachel flared at the last minute to kill some of her speed, brought her talons forward, and sailed through the open —

TSAPPPPP!

<Break off! Cassie, break off!>

Cassie was already reacting. She opened her wings, yanked a hard right, and skimmed within inches of the rough stucco wall of the mansion.

<Rachel!> I yelled. <Rachel!>

She had gone through the window. She was inside. But she wasn't answering. And with my falcon's eyes I could just make out a dim shape lying sprawled on the floor of the room inside.

Rachel was unconscious.

At least, I hoped she was only unconscious.

CHAPTER 16

Rachel! Trapped!

<Sheer off! Everyone back! Get altitude!>

BRRRRRRINNNNNNNNGGGG!

ScreeeeEEEE! ScreeeeEEEE! ScreeeeEEEE!

Alarms were ringing. A siren shrieked. I heard men's voices shouting.

I saw Cassie shoot high up, passing the top of the wall to keep her momentum. But Marco and Ax were struggling with dead air. So was I. I flapped hard, but the air down that close to the ground was still and cool. I flapped harder and rose, but slowly. Too slowly.

"Shoot them!"

"What, the birds?"

"Yes! The birds! Those are the orders!"

BLAM! BLAM! BLAM!

<Prince Jake!> Ax cried out, <I have been hit!>

I saw the northern harrier stagger in the air and start to fall. Could I reach him before he hit the ground?

<Hold on, Ax-man, I'm coming,> Tobias said. He was the only one of us with any altitude. Down he came in a mad, suicidal stoop, plunging toward the ground.

Ax had been thirty feet in the air when he started falling. Tobias was fifty feet up. It was impossible!

But down Tobias went, like a reddish bullet. He caught up with Ax when Ax's fluttering body was three feet from hitting the ground.

<This is gonna hurt!> Tobias yelled. He sank his talons into Ax's shoulder and chest, opened his wings, and swept down along the falling slope of the lawn, never more than an inch from disaster.

Cassie was rushing to help. She grabbed one of Ax's wings and she and Tobias managed to drag and haul the injured Andalite over the inner fence and the second fence. But they dropped him in the dog run.

A team of Rottweilers came tearing for him.

The dogs were racing, salivating, their big jowls shaking. Their trainer followed more slowly, unlimbering a submachine gun.

<Cassie! Tobias! Now or never!> I yelled as I went into a shallow dive. Too shallow, too slow. The dogs were sure to see me coming. But I aimed right for them. Right for the eyes of the nearest animal. I swept my talons forward.

The dog caught sight of me out of the corner of his eye. He turned! I struck!

Snap! A massive, crushing jaw closed over my left wing tip. But the teeth found nothing but feathers. I hit the grass, rolling. The dog came after me. In three bounds he'd have me. I was helpless.

Then something rocketed down, just behind me: a second osprey! Marco!

Marco raked the dog from behind, tearing a red line up the back of the dog's neck.

ROOWWWRR!

The dog spun, Marco flapped away, and I worked like a madman to get off the ground.

But the second dog had kept his focus on Tobias, Cassie, and Ax. Tobias and Cassie were flapping madly, dragging Ax's tattered bird body along the grass. They would almost get off the ground, then slip back. The dog was on them.

<Leave him!> I yelled.

<No way!> Tobias cried.

<Do it! Do it or you're all dead!>

Tobias and Cassie released Ax's body. They

fluttered away and the dog ran straight to the injured Ax and snatched him up in his jaws.

"Keep! Keep, Achilles!" the dog handler yelled.

With my keen vision I saw the dog freeze his jaw. He held Ax but did not bite down.

<What do we do?> Cassie cried.

<Get out of here! Move! Move!> I yelled.

I caught a slight breeze and soared up and away. Armed men and more dogs encircled Ax.

Through the supposedly open window of the house, I saw other men running to surround Rachel.

Two of us captured. And I was to blame.

CHAPTER 17

We joined up, those of us who were left, on the roof of a Wendy's a quarter mile away. We hid there behind rooftop air conditioners and exhaust fans, amid the smell of grease and the rippling heat.

<How long have we been in morph?> I asked.

<I don't know,> Marco yelled. <How am I supposed to know?>

<We could have gotten Ax out of there!> Tobias accused.

<They have Rachel and Ax,> Cassie said frantically. <We have to get them back!>

It was panic. No one thinking clearly.

I tried to focus. But the air conditioners were

roaring. The stink of frying burgers and onions and ketchup was overpowering.

<I think . . . I think we've been in morph about thirty minutes,> I said. <We have an hour and a half.>

<To do what?> Tobias demanded. <That place is a fortress! Fences, dogs, and some kind of force field in the windows.>

<Controllers,> Marco said. <Fenestre is a Controller. It was a trap. Has to be. Who else would shoot at birds?>

<Rachel and Ax will have to demorph in less than an hour and a half or be trapped,> Cassie said. <An hour and a half. That's how long we have. If they demorph surrounded by Controllers . . . I mean, they'll know Rachel is human, which means they'll figure out that we're all human. All except Ax.>

<I know,> I said. Actually, it was worse than that. See, Rachel knew she couldn't demorph where she could be seen by Controllers. If I knew Rachel, she'd rather be trapped forever in her eagle's body than let the truth out. She knew that if the Yeerks ever learned we were humans, not some bunch of renegade Andalites, our days were numbered. In low numbers.

<Being trapped in eagle form may not be the worst thing facing Rachel,> Tobias said.

<Oh, yeah, *you'd* think that!> Marco sneered with savage sarcasm. <Maybe Rachel doesn't want to spend the rest of her life eating mice and living in trees like you, Tobias.>

<That's not what I meant,> Tobias snapped back. <I meant she may not be alive. Or the body she's trapped in may be injured beyond saving.>

<Ax was alive, I'm sure of that,> Cassie said, a bit calmer than the other two.

<Didn't any of this show up when you researched this lunatic's mansion?> Marco demanded of me.

I didn't answer. I had to think. Time was running out. Tobias and Marco were at each other's throats. Cassie was starting to moan about how they'd find her parents, sooner or later. How once they had Rachel it was only a matter of time.

I had to make a plan. But who was I to be making plans? I'd led everyone into a disaster. Rachel . . . Ax . . . all of us, maybe.

<I don't know what to do.> It came out as a sob. I hadn't planned it. Hadn't meant to say it.

<What?> Tobias said.

<Ticktock, ticktock,> Marco said angrily. <We need a plan. Time is running out!>

<I don't have a plan, all right?!> I yelled.

<Don't give me that,> Marco shouted in my head. <You got us into this, now get us out!>

<Leave him alone,> Cassie said, coming to my defense.

But Marco's words had been spears aimed right at my heart. And Cassie defending me just made things worse.

My mind was split in two. Part of it was racing like an Indy car whose engine is ready to explode. Another part of it was swimming through molasses, stuck on the awful fact that Marco was right. I had failed my friends.

<We . . . we could use cockroach morphs,> Cassie said. <Crawl into the mansion and —>

<No time,> Marco said. <We'd have to morph way outside the outer fence, then get all the way up the hill, hundreds of yards. Besides, they're Controllers in there. They'll be ready for us now.>

<No,> I said suddenly.

<No, *what?*> Tobias said.

<They aren't Controllers,> I said, suddenly absolutely sure. <Any time we've ever gone after the Yeerks they may have used a lot of human-Controllers. But backing them up were always Hork-Bajir. No Hork-Bajir. And everyone used guns. Plain old, everyday guns. And dogs. The Yeerks wouldn't use dogs.>

<What kind of a human being would tell his guards to shoot birds?> Marco demanded.

<I don't know. But these are humans. Just humans. But Rachel and Ax may not know that.

We have to get them out of there. And we don't have time to be subtle.>

<They still have guns,> Cassie pointed out. <They may not have Dracon beams or squadrons of Hork-Bajir, but they still have guns and fences and dogs and probably some big, thick doors.>

<Yeah, they do,> I agreed. <And we don't have any morphs between us that are fast enough, and tough enough to bust into that place without getting shot up. But I have an idea. How far are we from The Gardens?>

CHAPTER 18

I flew as fast as my falcon body could carry me, which was pretty fast. But the wind was against me. I tried to tell myself it would all work out because on the way back the wind would be with me. But who can tell with the wind?

I left Marco and Cassie behind to keep an eye on things. I gave them instructions to do nothing. I didn't want us to get back and find they were captured, too.

But who was I to be giving anyone orders? I'd led my friends into a trap. A trap I might have expected if I'd taken the time to do some research. But no, I'd spent the night wasting time with my family.

Cassie had been right all along. We should

have tried to save Gump. That would have been the easy thing to do. Instead I had to try and play the big general and decide to go after Fenestre, even without any preparation.

Tobias flew with me to The Gardens. I wanted to be alone, really, but Tobias is a hundred times more experienced than any of us in the air. He knew the winds and clouds and thermals. He could help me fly faster.

We'd had less than an hour and a half. By the time we were flying above the animal habitats of The Gardens, we would have less than an hour. Half an hour to get back. That left half an hour to do what I had come to do, and to rescue Rachel and Ax back at the mansion.

There was no time to waste.

<Are you going to tell me what we're here for?> Tobias grumbled.

<Right down there,> I said.

Below us was an outdoor habitat of mixed grasses, a muddy wallow, and a water hole. Four shapes were visible in the habitat. Four large shapes that looked like fugitives from the age of dinosaurs.

<Rhinos?> Tobias asked incredulously.

<Yeah. I need a morph that can go straight through those fences, through the doors, and take a couple of bullets if need be. You have a better idea?>

<Nope. Not me. But how are you going to get close enough to acquire one of those things?>

<Two of the rhinos are off at the far end of the habitat. The crowds may not able to see them all that well.>

<You're just going to go right in?>

<There's no time for anything else.>

<Oh, man. Look, at least let me provide a distraction.>

I hesitated. Tobias was waiting for me to say yes or no. What if I was wrong? Again? Still, I could use a distraction. <Yeah, okay. But don't get hurt. You hear? Do not get hurt.>

Tobias peeled off and I floated down, down, like going down a spiral staircase. I aimed right for the broad back of the biggest rhinoceros. I flared my wings, reached out with my talons, and landed as gently as I could.

The big beast barely twitched.

I stood there, balanced on his back, my talons holding lightly to the thick old gray leather. So far, so good. But you can't acquire new DNA when you're in a morph. I had to be human to do it. And that was going to be tricky.

I looked off toward the high railing where people were watching the rhinos meander. With my falcon vision, they seemed shockingly close. I could see the color of their eyes. I could see a loose button on one guy's shirt. Of course, they only had human eyes. They couldn't see nearly as well as I could.

It doesn't matter, I told myself grimly. *No time to worry. Do it.*

I began to demorph. On the rhino's back. My falcon feathers began to melt and run together, confusing their neat geometric patterns. My talons grew less sharp, thicker, clumsier, with extra toes beginning to grow. I heard a deep, internal grinding sound as my human bones began to stretch out of the hollow bird bones.

I was already twice as heavy on the rhinoceros's back. Would he throw me off and trample me? No time to worry. Would the people notice what was happening? No time to worry. I had to trust Tobias.

And that's when I saw him swoop down from the sky and snatch a cotton candy from a little girl's hand as easily as he snatched mice from the grass.

Swooop! And off he went with the bright pink fluff ball. The girl yelled, the people around all gaped and laughed and pointed. Tobias began to put on an aerial display worthy of the Blue Angels at an air show.

No one was watching me as my lumpy human shape emerged from the sleek falcon's body. But I was still on the back of the rhino. On the back of a two-thousand-pound behemoth with a three-foot-long horn.

The rhino moved! But he was just ambling over to greener grass.

I continued to demorph. Then, all of a sudden, the rhino noticed.

"Ffmraha!" he snorted. He broke into a trot. I had no hands yet. No talons anymore, either. I rolled off and lay face down in the dust.

Come on, Jake, morph!

The rhinoceros towered above me. It was like lying down on the ground beside a truck. He blinked one eye at me. And then he lowered his massive horn.

Sniff. Sniff.

That face, that horn, hovered inches from me, as the rhinoceros sniffed me and I prayed he wouldn't impale me. He was growing more agitated. He was upset by what he was watching. No surprise. It would have upset me, too, watching a boy squirm and mutate his way out of a bird.

And then I had a hand. I stuck it out, half-blind, and touched the horn. I wrapped my still-emerging fingers halfway round it, and I focused with all my mind.

When you acquire animals, they go into a sort of trance. Except sometimes they don't. And if this was one of those times, the rhino would trample me and use me for target practice with his horn.

I focused on the beast. I focused and felt him become a part of me.

CHAPTER 19

We raced back from The Gardens. I was exhausted. Tobias was exhausted. We had no choice. Time was running out.

The wind had shifted. It wasn't in our faces, but it was strong from the south and we were flying west. We kept having to fight our way back on course.

Marco and Cassie were waiting in the trees across the road from Fenestre's front gate. Their time in morph was short, too. As short as Rachel's and Ax's time.

<Marco! Cassie!> I yelled down. <Anything happen?>

<Yeah, the clock kept ticking,> Marco said.

<We noticed one thing,> Cassie said. <Thank

goodness for these eyes. We saw you were right not to try and sneak inside in some kind of insect morph. There's a band of poison around each door. And some kind of bug zapper in the windows. That must be what shocked Rachel. I think Mr. Fenestre has some psychological problems.>

<He can afford them,> Marco said. <Now what are we doing to get Rachel and Ax out of there?>

<I'm going to knock down the fences, kick in the door, and stomp anything or anyone that gets in my way,> I said.

<Cool.> Marco laughed with a touch of his now-strained humor. <Rachel would approve. But how?>

I landed on the ground at the base of the tree. <You guys get ready. I'm hoping Mr. Fenestre built that place with high ceilings and wide hallways.>

I demorphed as quickly as I could. I stayed in human form for only a few seconds, then focused my thoughts on the rhinoceros.

It is unbelievably tiring to morph rapidly like that. You feel like your body is running on one half-dead double-A battery. But I could be tired later, not now.

The first change was my skin. It went from delicate human of the pink variety, to something like inch-thick leather that's been out in the sun for ten years. It thickened and rippled all over. I was still human, but gray and massive. It was like wearing living armor.

My legs thickened and shortened. My fingers withered away. Only the fingernails remained and they became hard and big as irons. I fell forward onto all fours, a growing mass of gray, like molten steel bubbling and reforming.

I felt my ears crawl up the side of my head. They elongated, then curled to form open tubes.

And then, last of all, my face. My entire face simply began to stretch. Out and out and out. The bones of my face and skull grew, multiplied, thickened. It was as if some busy crew of engineers were rebuilding my face, always saying, "We need more here, more support there, more armor, more strength."

My head was gigantic!

<What the . . . what are you morphing?!> Marco asked.

And then, growing from the far end of my monstrously big head, the horns began to emerge.

A smaller one toward the back that grew, then stopped. And the larger horn. The one that grew and grew and grew. My eyesight was dim and badly focused, but I could see the horn sprout. Up and up it went. Thicker, larger, longer.

<Oh,> Marco said. <*That's* what you're morphing.>

<How much time?> I asked.

<Maybe ten minutes,> Tobias said.

I felt the rhino's mind emerge beneath my own human consciousness. It was not what I'd expected. This mind was not violent. In fact, the dominant instinct seemed to be simple hunger. The rhino wanted to graze.

But beneath that placid herbivore consciousness there was something else. Not aggression, but defensiveness. Not fear, but concern. The rhino had to be careful, lest it was challenged by another rhinoceros.

The incredibly dim and almost useless eyes searched for a shape vaguely like its own. The ears twisted and turned, aiming at each new sound, looking for the sounds of another rhino. The excellent nose sniffed the air.

No challengers. No enemies. Just some birds. The rhino was calm.

I would have to supply the aggression. Which was fine, because I had plenty. I had to save Rachel and Ax. And I had to do it right now.

<Okay, you guys stay with me, but stay back. Wait till I've cleared away defenses before you advance. Now, let's see what this horn can do.>

CHAPTER 20

My new body moved surprisingly well. I felt almost like I was tiptoeing. But I was a tiptoeing giant.

I trotted out from beneath the cover of the trees. I knew the gate of Fenestre's compound was right across the street. But I could not see the gate. I couldn't see anything beyond maybe thirty yards, and then, only if it moved. In order to see, I had to look first with one eye, then the other, because the two eyes were too far apart, with too much massive jaw and snout and horn separating them. It was like having your eyes in different rooms.

<You guys will have to aim me,> I said.

109

<A little left,> Marco said. <That's it. Now, forward!>

I trotted. I broke into a run. I felt hard pavement beneath my surprisingly sensitive feet.

<Gate!> Marco yelled.

I lowered my horn. I increased my speed. The gate was metal bars. I saw them clearly about two seconds before I hit them.

More than two thousand pounds of rhino hit tempered steel.

WHAM!

I felt the impact in my massive, bony face and back into my shoulders. It was like getting hit in the face with a sledgehammer! But it was like getting hit and not caring. I felt the impact. But my rhinoceros body was used to impact. It was built for impact.

<What happened to the gate?> I asked, too blind to be sure.

<What gate?> Marco said. <Okay, now straight on, veering slightly right, big guy!>

I trotted on my four Greek column legs. I felt the twisted remains of the gate as I ran across them.

ScrrrEEEET! ScrrrEEEET!

<Man, does this guy have a lot of different alarms, or what?> Tobias said.

<Okay, fence number two,> Marco announced.

I kept running. This time it was just chain link. I felt something sort of tug at my horn.

<Where's the fence?> I asked.

<You just went through it,> Cassie said.

<All right. This may work,> Marco said.

"Rowrrrowrrrowrr!" I heard the dogs very clearly. Smelled them even more clearly.

<Doggies!> Tobias warned.

I caught a vague glimpse of two dark shapes hurtling through the air toward me. I think maybe they tried to bite me. I'm not sure. I did feel a sort of scraping sensation on one side.

"Yow! Yow! Yow! Yowyowyowyow!"

<What happened to the dogs?> I asked.

<Doggies go bye-bye,> Marco said with a laugh. <The doggies are hauling doggie butt.>

<I think I like this morph,> I said. <What's next?>

<Final fence, then the door.>

<Look out! Guards! The guys with the shot-guns!>

"Holy crap!" I heard someone yell. "What is that?"

"Shoot it!"

I spotted them moving. It was like watching a very old, very fuzzy black-and-white movie on a bad TV. They were shadows, ghosts moving swiftly against a blurry background. Just enough for me to see.

I turned toward them, all rhino instinct now. They were possible danger. They were challenging me. That was a mistake.

BLAM! BLAM! BLAM!

Rhinos get shot at all the time. Unfortunately, there are people stupid enough to think rhino horn is a medicine, and people creepy enough to slaughter endangered rhinos to get it.

But they don't go hunting rhinoceros with shotguns. You want to shoot a rhino, you need a high-power, high-caliber rifle. Not a shotgun that fires a bunch of small pellets.

BLAM! BLAM!

I felt something sting my face and shoulders. It made me mad. I charged. Not a trot, an out-and-out run, with head down and horn out.

"Run!"

They ran. I ran after them. It took about three seconds for me to catch the first one. I plowed right into him, felt the contact with his soft, mushy body, tossed my head, and . . .

. . . Let's just say that particular man won't be sitting down for a long, long time.

I had lost the other guard. But that was okay. They weren't my goal.

<Get me to the door!> I yelled to the others.

<Left . . . okay, now right . . . okay now . . . jeez, what are you, blind? Left, right, okay, CHARGE!>

I charged.

WHAMMMM!

I felt like I'd hit a truck. I backed up and slammed forward again.

WHAMMMM! Crunch.

<Man, that was a tough door!> I said.

<Um, Jake? You missed the door. That was the wall. You okay?> Cassie asked.

<I'm fine. One more push and we'll be in.> I reared back and slammed forward. I felt scraping along my back. Then I was in much cooler air.

<We're inside, aren't we?> I asked.

<Yes,> Tobias answered, sounding tense. <And we are out of time.>

CHAPTER 21

I'm sure it was a beautiful house. But I didn't really see it. All I saw with my dim rhino-vision were walls and doorways. But at least we'd been right to guess that there were wide hall-ways. Wide enough for me to barrel down like a . . . well, like a rhinoceros.

And the ceilings were high enough that To-bias, Cassie, and Marco could fly down them, searching madly from room to room. Searching with vision greater than human vision and hear-ing that could pick up the sound of a gopher belching from a distance the length of a football field.

They used me to open doors.

<Jake, open this door,> Marco would say. I'd

turn where he showed me, shove my massive bony face forward, and the door would explode in splinters.

Crrrr-UNCH-Bang!

<We are trashing this man's home,> Cassie said. <I sure hope he is a Controller after all this.>

<He can afford to have his doors fixed,> Marco said.

<That's not the point,> Cassie said. Then, <Jake, open this door, please.>

Crrrr-UNCH-bang!

<Nothing,> Tobias complained. <Nothing, nothing, nothing! Nothing in any of these rooms, and there may be a hundred rooms in this place.>

<Tobias is right. We are out of time,> Cassie said.

<This isn't the way to do it,> I said. <We can't just search room-to-room. It could take hours. We need to figure this out. How do we find Ax and Rachel? Where would they be?>

<In the last place we look,> Marco grumbled. <Or at least . . . wait a minute! Wherever they are, they'll be guarded.>

<Yes!> I said. <Of course. We just rampage till we see something well guarded.>

<I'll head upstairs,> Tobias said.

He zoomed away and up a large staircase. I

lumbered along into a vast open living room area. I stomped on through. I tried not to crush too much furniture, but I was big and half-blind, so I kept hearing the crunch of wood and the shatter of glass and pottery in my wake.

<Up here!> Tobias yelled.

Then, not as loud as before, but still loud enough . . . BLAM! BLAM!

<Tobias!>

<I'm okay! But I found an area with two big guys with big guns. It's upstairs.>

I tried to turn around and head back to the stairs, but then Marco yelled.

<Uh-oh! Guys coming up behind us. Man, how many gunmen does this lunatic hire? Jake, we have to go *through* these guys to get back to the stairs!>

<I got guys on my tail!> Tobias yelled down from upstairs.

I spun around and wiped out a couch in the process. <This way?!>

<No, a little left!>

I turned and annihilated a coffee table. Then I charged. I couldn't tell the difference between the men and various pole lamps and bookcases, except when they moved. The blur drew my eye, and I smelled humans.

I lowered my head and charged.

BLAM! BLAM!

Shotgun pellets stung but didn't penetrate beneath my outer skin.

POP! POP! POP! POP!

I was hit. I staggered. I felt the bullet from the handgun tear into my right shoulder. A second slug lodged in the bone of my face.

I hit the guy with the gun. I was mad. I lowered my horn and I tossed my head back. He went flying back over my shoulder.

"Ya-ah-AHHHHHH!"

The other man jumped aside. I think he was fumbling to reload his shotgun. I sideswiped him and knocked him into the wall. Then I was out of the room, back into the hallway, tearing along back to the staircase.

I was bleeding. And I was weakening on my right side. My right front leg was moving slower. The bullet in my face must have ricocheted off. I felt pain there, but not the heaviness I felt in my shoulder.

I came to the stairs and tried to charge straight up. But rhinos were never meant for climbing stairs. My legs wouldn't lift high enough. My weight and momentum were too much. The wooden stairs splintered.

BLAM! BLAM!

<Tobias! What's going on up there?>

<I'm leading these guys around in circles and they're blowing the crap out the wall and ceiling trying to shoot me.>

<I can't make the stairs. We need more fire-power. Marco, Cassie, morph! Tobias, keep it up. Keep leading 'em on.>

A bird trapped in a house, being chased by two guys with shotguns. Had I just sentenced Tobias to death?

I started to demorph as fast as I could. But while my thought-speak was still functioning, something occurred to me. <Rachel! Ax! Can you guys hear me? Rachel! Ax!>

<. . . unh . . . what?>

<Who is that?>

<. . . unh . . . it is me, Aximili,> Ax said.

He sounded dazed. I wasn't surprised. <Ax! Demorph! Time's up!>

<But there are humans here watching me, Prince Jake.>

Another decision. <Just do it, Ax, we're coming for you! Do you —> My thought-speak went dead as I became more human than rhinoceros.

<Yes, Prince Ja —> Ax fell silent.

I was shrinking. My armored flesh became tender human skin. My face was flat and delicate. But my legs could handle stairs. I still heard the sounds of gunfire from upstairs. And the sad thing was, I was glad. As long as they were still shooting, it meant Tobias wasn't dead yet.

Marco and Cassie were just becoming human again. They were three-foot-tall lumps of feathers and shrinking beaks and emerging skin.

One wrong move and Tobias was gone. Ax might be demorphing in front of people who might be Controllers. Rachel . . . no one knew whether Rachel was even conscious and capable of demorphing. Or alive at all. And now the three of us were utterly vulnerable, weak, pathetic.

I just kept thinking: This wasn't even supposed to be a very dangerous mission. And now, we were as close to being wiped out as we'd ever been.

"Cshom on!" I said, slurring my words with a mouth that was not yet human. "No chime kleft!"

I started up the stairs, staggering on my shifting, changing legs. The joints weren't right. The toes weren't toes, and my ankles seemed to have no flexibility. But time was up. I dragged myself up those stairs, hoping desperately that I had not killed us all.

CHAPTER 22

I was human by the time I had reached the top of the stairs. But human isn't a great morph when you're thinking about going against guys with guns.

As I ran I saw, to my horror, something emerge from the flesh of my shoulder. About as big as a fingertip, smashed, the color of mud. It was the bullet that had lodged in my shoulder. By good luck it had ended up outside my body as it morphed into a smaller form.

The bullet dropped to the carpet.

A hawk zipped by overhead, scraping the walls with its wings. A loose feather drifted down.

<What are you guys doing, looking like that?> Tobias demanded.

"Are they still after you?"

<Yeah, but I lost them temporarily. The room they were guarding is down the hall, then through this big, massive bedroom. You'll see a doorway. Last time I went past, there were still a couple of guys guarding it.>

"What do we do?" Marco asked.

I swear, I almost punched him. If one more person asked me what to do . . .

"Morph again. Combat mode. Tobias? Try and reach Rachel and Ax with thought-speak. If you get Rachel, tell her to demorph right now, no arguing. If you get Ax, tell him to —"

<I hear my guys coming,> Tobias interrupted. <Into that side room! It's unlocked. I'll lead them away!>

Marco, Cassie, and I all dodged into the side room. I heard the sound of heavy, weary feet tramping by.

"Where is that lousy bird?"

"What I can't figure is why we're chasing it and blowing holes in the walls and ceiling."

"'Cause we want to keep our jobs, that's why," the first man muttered.

By the time they were gone, I was in tiger morph. The rhino was great for busting things down. But I wanted eyes and ears and reflexes to go along with my power. And nothing I'd ever morphed could do as much damage as the tiger.

Cassie had morphed a wolf, Marco a gorilla. In a fight they were our standard morphs.

<Rachel!> I yelled, as soon as my thought-speak was back. <Rachel! If you can hear me, demorph! Demorph now!> To Marco and Cassie I said, <Come on! Let's do this!>

Marco opened the door with his almost-human fingers and we ran. Down the hall, through a bedroom that I swear, without exaggeration, was as big as a basketball court, and up to the doorway, where two very scared-looking guys stood cradling weapons.

One carried a shotgun. The other a small submachine gun. They were thirty feet away. For a frozen moment, no one moved.

I could cover thirty feet in two seconds.

In those same two seconds, the guy with the machine gun could fire ten rounds. He could easily kill me. If he failed, the force of my leap, my desperate need to defend myself, would ensure that he died.

It was time to gamble. <Look, you two men . . .>

They stared at me like they were going nuts. They could guess that it was me they were hearing in their heads. But they had never even imagined talking to a tiger before.

Then again, they'd never expected to be face-to-face with a small, angry zoo, either.

<Yes, it's me, the tiger. Don't worry about how

or why. Here's all you need to know: I don't want to hurt you. But I have to go past you. You may shoot me, but you won't kill me fast enough to keep me from taking you down. See this paw?>

I lifted one paw. My tiger paws are about as big around as a frying pan. I extended the cruel, yellowed claws.

<With this paw, I can literally knock your heads from your shoulders and send them rolling like bowling balls. Now, I don't know what you're getting paid for this job —>

"Not enough," said the man with the machine gun. "I can't believe I'm talking to animals. But that tiger makes sense."

"We're not getting paid nearly enough," his partner agreed. "We put down our weapons and walk away. Agreed, Mr. Tiger?"

<Agreed. Cassie? Keep an eye on them.>

Cassie trained her acute wolf senses on the men. If they had even thought about trying anything tricky, she'd have known it before they did.

<Marco? Now it's your turn to open a door. Open that door.>

Marco raised his huge gorilla arms back over his head, preparing to swing them down with shattering force.

<Marco? Try the knob first.>

<Oh.>

He opened the door. And I leaped through.

CHAPTER 23

I bounded into the room. It was dark, but my tiger's eyes could see through the gloom as easily as if it had been lit with stadium lights.

There seemed to be a sky overhead. Green, mostly, with vivid flashes of lightning. Scruffy plants grew from what seemed to be soil beneath my feet. And in the center of the room, perhaps fifteen feet across, was a shallow pond of liquid the color and consistency of molten lead.

There were two cages beside the pool. Ax was in one. He was halfway between his northern harrier morph and his own Andalite body. He was frozen stiff. Unmoving. Not even breathing, like some nightmare statue composed of gray feathers and a scorpion tail and talons and a mouth-less face.

In the other cage was Rachel. Still a bald eagle.

My tiger eyes were very good. My tiger ears were good, too. I heard no heartbeat from her. I saw no slight movement of her chest rising and falling with breathing.

I felt my heart stop beating for several long seconds. Dead. Both dead. I'd been too late.

There was a man there, too. I recognized the face. Joe Bob Fenestre, the second richest man on earth. Head of Web Access America.

I recognized what he had in his hand, too: a Yeerk Dracon beam. He was not pointing it at me. He was pointing it at Ax.

Wrong again, Jake. This man was a Controller. Had to be.

Marco and Cassie came in behind me. After a few moments Tobias joined us. But Fenestre just kept staring at me.

At last he spoke. "So. Not Yeerks, after all. I'm to be destroyed by Andalites. Well, I suppose there is some honor in that, at least."

<Let my friends go,> I said harshly.

He shrugged. "You can take them. I don't care. Killing Andalites is not my life anymore."

<Yeah? My friends *look* dead,> I said.

125

He frowned. "Nonsense. Don't you recognize bio-stasis when you see it? They are simply frozen in time. I thought you Andalites were supposed to be so advanced when it comes to technology."

My heart quickened. Bio-stasis? What was that?

<Get them out of there,> I said.

"Or what?" he mocked. "You'll kill me? You'll kill me anyway."

I was panting. My mind was racing madly. What game was this man playing? How could I win? <Why would I kill you?>

"I'm a Yeerk," he said. "A Controller. Although my host and I are on very good terms. I made him rich. I wrote his famous Web browser. We've been partners all these years."

<Yeerks don't have partners,> I said.

He laughed. "No," he drawled, "we don't." He looked at me with a sharp, shrewd look. "Who sent you after me? Have you made some kind of deal with my brother?"

<Your brother?>

"You are obviously Andalites," he said patiently. "No one else has your amazing morphing technology. But I have to ask myself, why would Andalites go to so much trouble to kill me? Me, of all Yeerks?"

I was totally confused. I hesitated.

<This is weird,> Marco said, sending me a private thought-speak message.

<This guy is cornered,> Cassie said. <He thinks he's toast. You can see it in his eyes. We need to find out more.>

I paced a little. Tigers get restless just standing. Should I take a chance? Should I tell him at least some of the truth?

<We traced you here from the Web page. The one about Yeerks.>

He nodded. "Yes, but why come after . . . ?" His face lit up. "Of course! You were looking for allies! You weren't sure, were you? You thought perhaps it was all real, that humans were forming a resistance to the Yeerk invasion of their planet! You came here to see if I was for you, or against you!"

Then he began to laugh. He laughed in that sick way people do when they're laughing but nothing is funny.

"Shall I tell you who and what I am, Andalite? Shall I?"

I didn't answer. I waited.

"My Yeerk designation is Esplin-Nine-Four-Double-Six. Note the 'double six.' Do you know what it means?"

<No.>

"A 'double' designation means that I am a twin. That two Yeerks grew from the same grub.

When there are twins, one is considered the prime, and one the lesser. I am the lesser. My brother, my twin, is the prime. To him go the best assignments, the best hosts, the rank, the power, the glory. And to me, only what I can take."

He made a fist on the word "take."

"In some cases, brothers can share. In some cases, twins can even become allies. But not with my brother. My brother is power mad. Or maybe just mad now. He left me nothing. He assigned me to a poor, unimportant human host. This Joe Bob Fenestre, a lowly programmer working in the bowels of a telephone company.

"Well, that wasn't good enough. I wanted more. And if I couldn't have it as a Yeerk, I'd have it as a human. I ended up making an alliance with my host. We were two of a kind. Two losers in the shadow of our betters. I used Yeerk technical knowledge to make Fenestre rich. And in the process, I created Web Access America, which made me the greatest source of information on humans there was. I knew secrets my brother could only guess at."

<You sift E-mail. You spy on chat rooms.>

"You know human computer terminology," he said.

I swallowed hard. I'd been careless. I had sounded "human." Bluff it out. <We Andalites

are a small, hunted band on this planet. Knowledge is survival.>

He seemed satisfied with that.

"I became an invaluable asset to the invasion. All by myself I had become a powerful human with vast information. But of course, my brother couldn't tolerate that. He had me declared a traitor. He cut me off from the Kandrona. He would have killed me. For the crime of being as great as he, he'd have murdered me."

Joe Bob Fenestre's eyes bored into me. And I felt a chill of premonition. See, right then I knew who this twin brother was. Who he *had* to be.

<Oh, my God,> Cassie whispered. She'd guessed, too.

"Yes, only one twin can be great," Fenestre said bitterly. "Only one of us could be the mighty Visser Three."

CHAPTER 24

We first encountered Visser Three within minutes of finding the Andalite prince, Elfangor.

Visser Three showed up and murdered the helpless Elfangor. Since that time we have fought him many times. He is the only Yeerk in all the universe ever to have successfully taken over an Andalite body, long ago in another war on another planet. When he took the Andalite body as a host, he acquired the Andalite's ability to morph. He is the only morph-capable Yeerk.

And now I understood why his brother, this Yeerk living in the head of Joe Bob Fenestre, would instruct his men to shoot at birds and any other animal they saw. Any one of them might be Visser Three in morph.

"I gather, from your silence, that you know my brother," Fenestre said.

<We have fought him,> I said simply.

"And yet, you're still alive. Not many can say that. My compliments."

<How do you survive without having access to the Yeerk pool? I see you have created a replica here in this room, but surely you haven't managed to create your own Kandrona to supply the vital Kandrona rays.>

Fenestre nodded. "Well, well. So you know a Yeerk pool when you see one. And you know about the Kandrona." He shrugged. "I have found a way to stay alive without a Kandrona. That's not important. What's important is . . . what now?"

<He's lying,> Cassie whispered instantly. <Or at least he's not telling the whole truth. The Kandrona. He doesn't want to talk about that.>

I nodded my tiger head. It probably looked funny, such a human gesture coming from the huge cat. <Your brother must know where you are. He could kill you anytime he wants. He could hit you from orbit and leave this place a big, smoky ruin.>

"No, no, that would be too noisy. Some idiot human with a camcorder could manage to record it."

<He could send in Hork-Bajir. They'd cut

through your guards just like we did. Or he could come himself. If he wanted to kill you, he would. He could. He hasn't. So why not?>

Fenestre smiled a wintry smile. "Clever, clever Andalites. So good with your computers and your magnificent Dome ships. You still think you're the lords of the galaxy, don't you? We spread from planet to planet and you keep falling back. And yet your arrogance is so unbelievable you never pause to consider that maybe you're not so clever, after all."

<Cassie's right,> Marco chimed in. <He's weaseling. He's trying to distract you.>

<Yeah, you're both right,> I said. Then to Fenestre I said, <If you want to live, answer my questions. Answer me, and you'll live. Lie . . .> I let the threat hang in the air.

Fenestre looked at me long and hard. "I suppose I'll have to rely on Andalite honor," he said in a mocking tone. "All right. My brother has not killed me because I have information he wants and needs. He doesn't want me dead, he wants me in his torture chamber aboard his Blade ship. You see, I have found a way to survive without the Kandrona. And Visser Three would give anything to know how."

Fenestre lowered the Dracon beam he'd been pointing at Ax. "There's a way to process and refine Kandrona rays from another source. It can be made into an edible product. A food, so to speak, that I can consume with my human mouth and digest."

I felt a cold chill. If that was true, there would be no stopping the Yeerks. Their reliance on Yeerk pools and Kandrona rays was one of their greatest weaknesses.

<You're lying,> I said. <If there was a way to keep Yeerks alive without Kandrona rays and Yeerk pools, that information would make you invulnerable, even to your brother.>

This time the wintry smile was even colder. If that's possible. "Oh, maybe not. For one thing, there is a long, involved process. But that's not the problem. The problem is the raw material. The raw material is my brother Yeerks. I must destroy and process and consume a Yeerk every three days to survive. I have become a cannibal."

<Whoa,> Marco said.

"My brother would use this process for himself. But, as you can imagine, it would never become popular around the Yeerk Empire."

<You really are Visser Three's twin,> I said. I felt sick. Then I felt sicker. <How do you get the Yeerks?>

He shrugged. "What do you think that silly Yeerk forum is about, that silly mix of fact and fiction? I control Web Access America. I know the identity of all the screen names. The chat room is full of different types: people who are actually Controllers, trying to throw suspicious humans offtrack; humans who have discovered our little invasion and are trying to rally opposition to us; and then, there's me. I spot the Controllers. I spot the humans who think they have found family members who are Yeerks. I monitor the real gung ho Yeerk-fighters who identify potential Controllers. I track down the screen names. I find the Yeerks. One every three days. Ten a month."

<Cool by me,> Marco whispered. <Give the man a pat on the back, and let's get Ax and Rachel outta here.>

I had the same feeling. Fenestre was a sickening creature, but as vile as he might be, he was wiping out a hundred or more Yeerks per year. So much the better.

But then Cassie exploded. <How are you getting the Yeerks from the human hosts?!>

Fenestre cocked an eyebrow at her. He seemed surprised. I saw a shadow of suspicion in his eyes. Cassie's question had not been whispered. It had been shouted angrily.

Why, he was asking himself, *would an Andalite care?*

"How am I getting the Yeerks from their human hosts?" His face was dark. His eyes empty. "How do you think I get them?"

CHAPTER 25

Cassie let loose a growl and was racing toward Fenestre before I could say a word. He raised his Dracon beam. I leaped through the air.

I landed, paws outstretched but claws retracted, on Cassie. I knocked her wolf body sprawling across the floor.

<What are you doing?!> she yelled.

<We aren't here to annihilate this guy,> I said. <I told him we wouldn't.>

<Do you know what he's doing? Do you understand?> Cassie cried.

<I know. I know. I KNOW!> I screamed in frustration. <But I told him he was safe. I promised. Besides . . .>

<No! Don't say it, Jake. If you say that I won't

be able to deal with you anymore. So *don't* say it.>

I felt like she'd punched me. In my own, real face. What had I been about to say? Was I really going to say it was okay for this creature to go on doing what he did, as long as he got the Yeerks?

Was I going to say that? Me?

<I wasn't going to say what you think,> I said lamely.

Cassie didn't answer. She's good at spotting lies. Too good.

<I . . . I don't think . . .> I stammered.

<That kid, Gump. That kid who was worried about his dad,> Cassie said. <That lonely little kid. That's who this monster goes after, Jake. Not some abstract person with no face and no name. He'll wait until Gump does something stupid. Till he confesses his fears to his Controller father, and his father makes *him* a Controller, too. Then Fenestre will go after them.>

<What do you expect me to do?> I asked her. <You want to get rid of this man because he's evil? Do you want to do it yourself, Cassie?>

<You . . . your morph would do it better,> she said.

<You want me to get rid of him for you?> I asked. <That's what you want?>

Fenestre just stood there, waiting, as a wolf and a tiger bristled, face-to-face. He was trying to figure something out. But I could see from his eyes that the truth had not come to him, yet.

I backed away from Cassie. I turned back to Fenestre. <My friend has lost friends in battle against your people. She is emotional.>

He nodded, unimpressed. "We've all lost friends in this unpleasantness."

<Release my two friends,> I said. <We'll let you live. We'll walk away. As long as you are in this house, we won't harm you. But I'll tell you so you'll know: If we ever catch up with you in the outside world, that protection will not exist.>

It was a stupid little threat. I said it to make myself feel better.

Ax and Rachel were released. The instant Fenestre turned off the bio-stasis fields, Ax continued to morph back into his normal Andalite shape.

I stared hard at Rachel. Was she breathing? Yes!

Was there still time to get her back into her own body?

<Rachel! Can you hear me?>

<Huh? What? Oh, man! What am I doing here?>

<Rachel, listen to me. Start demorphing. Right now.>

<There's some guy! Who's that guy?> she asked, glaring at Fenestre with eagle's eyes.

137

<Rachel, for once, don't argue. Forget the guy, we're getting out of here. Demorph! Do it! Marco. Get Rachel. Carry her out of here.>

<I'm not letting him carry me!>

But she was too weak to do much, so Marco went over and lifted her gently in his massive gorilla hands.

"Perhaps we'll meet again," Fenestre said cockily as we backed away.

I said nothing. What was there to say? I was letting a monster live. I was letting a killer go free.

By the time we hit the stairs Rachel was demorphing. Ax was almost fully Andalite. He still had two bird-shot pellets in his body, but they weren't enough to harm him.

Tobias flew, as well as he could, overhead. We stumbled and trotted down the stairs, through the wreckage of the house and outside into the fenced, defended yard.

By the time we reached the trees, Rachel was Rachel again. We all demorphed, and soon we were five tired, wary kids and one Andalite hidden in the deep shadows of the trees.

We could still see the house. Fenestre's billionaire mansion.

"What happened in there?" Rachel demanded. "Someone *ripped* that place. Was there some big fight and I missed it? Oh, man! I can't believe I missed a big fight. So what happened?"

"Someone will tell you later," I said shortly.

"Was the guy a Controller or not?" Rachel demanded. "Was he a good guy or a bad guy?"

I laughed a little. My eyes locked with Cassie's and then we both looked away, unwilling to make contact. "Rachel, I don't even know which *I* am anymore."

CHAPTER 26

I guess someone eventually told Rachel and Ax what had happened. It wasn't me.

I got home and went up to my room and just stared at nothing for a long time. My mom called me to dinner and I mumbled my way through.

And then I went out in the backyard and sat on my rusted-out old swing set from when I was four and I stared at the sky as it turned dark. The stars came out and man, I hated them. They weren't beautiful, they were deadly. It was from the stars that all my problems had come.

My mom came out after a while. She pretended like she was checking to see if the grass needed watering. But of course she was checking on me.

"Whatcha doing out here? Thinking great thoughts?"

"Nah. Just hanging."

She locked her arms over her chest and looked up at the sky like I was doing. "It's a beautiful night. Look at the stars."

"Yeah."

"Is anything bothering you, Jake?"

"Nope."

"Well, if anything was bothering you, you could probably tell me without my embarrassing you too much."

"I know, Mom. It's nothing."

She sighed. "Well, I guess it had to happen sooner or later. You've turned into a real teenager. Mom's too out of it to talk to."

She didn't say it in a mean way. More like a joke.

I made a smile for her. "That must be it," I said. "It must be that whole teenage thing."

She shrugged. "You know, when I was your age and feeling upset, my mother, your gram, would always just say, 'You don't know what un-happy is, you're just a kid.' Like anything a kid would feel would be less difficult or painful than what an adult would feel."

"That's probably true," I said, not really lis-tening.

"No, it isn't," my mother said firmly. "In a lot

of ways being a kid is worse than being an adult. You have the same things to deal with: friends, temptations, love and hate, and all that. Only you don't have the two great weapons that adults have to help them."

I cocked an eye at her. "What two great weapons?"

"Well, the first is experience. Experience maybe doesn't make you smarter, but it means you can think, 'Hey, I had something like this happen once before, and I survived.'"

"Okay, I'll ask: What's the second great weapon?"

She looked right at me. "You are, Jake. Because as your mom, I can look at you and think, 'Oh, man, as bad as I feel right now, as bad as things may be, at least it isn't as bad as being a teenager.'"

I laughed. It was a tired, weak laugh, but it was something.

"You know, *X-Files* is on. You used to love that show."

The next day at school I was still feeling bad. It's nice that my mom and dad care about me. It's nice that they sympathize. But they don't understand, and they can't understand because for them everything is about my age.

How can they help me make life-and-death

decisions? How can they help me keep making those decisions when I've made mistakes?

How can they help me make decisions no human being can ever make correctly — like deciding what to do with Fenestre?

I looked around for Cassie. We'd left it on pretty bad terms. But after a while I realized she wasn't there. Wasn't in school.

I suddenly knew where she was.

I made my way to the roof of the school building, cursing under my breath because I knew I was going to get busted for skipping second period. Then I morphed to my falcon and flew away.

I wasted some time going to Gump's house, which was stupid. Cassie would have waited till he was away from the house. So I searched around for the nearest elementary school and headed there.

The kids were at recess. One little boy was way off by himself at the far end of the playfield. There was a dog with him. At least, the average person walking by would think it was a dog. I knew it was a wolf.

As I watched, the little boy patted the wolf and then walked back to his classmates.

The wolf watched him go, then jumped the fence and faded toward some nearby trees.

<Cassie,> I said.

She looked up, surprised. I landed on the

ground and began to demorph. She resumed her human shape, too.

"That was Gump, I guess."

"Yeah."

"What did you tell him?"

"I told him I was a magic, talking wolf. He didn't exactly buy that. I guess by his age they're pretty much past the point where they believe in magic."

"Yeah, I guess so."

"I told him not to go to that chat room again. I told him . . ." Her lip quivered suddenly. "I told him not to talk to his father about Yeerks. Told him not to . . ." Her voice was strangled. She gritted her teeth and squeezed out the last few words. "I told that little boy not to trust his father."

There were tears running down her face. I guess they were running down my face, too. One of the things Cassie and I share is that we trust our parents, unlike some people, I guess.

"What a terrible thing for me to do," Cassie said. "What a filthy, disgusting thing for me to do."

"It was the best you could do," I said. "It was all you could do. I guess it's hard to fight evil without doing some along the way." Maybe there was a little "I told you so" in my voice.

Cassie just walked away. I let her go. Not

everything can be settled. Not everything can be smoothed over.

A few days later they showed a fire on the TV news. It was a very big story because it was this huge mansion.

The mansion belonged to billionaire Joe Bob Fenestre. Fenestre was safe. No one was hurt.

I remembered warning him that he was safe only as long as he stayed in that house. Now it was no longer possible for him to stay in the house.

Did the mansion burn down on its own? Or did someone start the fire that deprived that evil creature of sanctuary?

If someone set the fire, there was a long list of suspects. Visser Three. Cassie. One of the others.

Me.

I guess you'll never know.

I make mistakes. I fail sometimes. Sometimes I'm just plain stupid. Sometimes there is no right answer to the problems we face, but what can you do but keep trying to figure the answer out, anyway? What else can you do?

About a week went by after the fire before I went to Cassie's house. She was in the barn, taking care of the sick animals.

I didn't ask her any questions, and she didn't ask me. I helped her put a splint on a deer with a broken leg. It was nice because, you know, it was just a good thing to do, no second-guessing, no doubts.

And after a while Cassie and I started talking and even laughing. The others came over and we talked about flying. But instead of flying, we stayed there and shoveled the manure out of the barn.

The six of us shoveled dirty hay, and Marco made dumb jokes, and Ax tried to eat a cow pie, and Rachel moaned about Cassie's pathetic taste in clothing, and we were us again.

For now.

17 The Underground

<This was not easy to figure out,> Tobias said proudly. <Hours and hours of following known Controllers. Then I had to keep stealing peeks in through the windows. I even morphed to human to check out the inside. That's how I found out about the Happy Meal.>

We were flies. The six of us. We were zipping madly around inside a McDonald's. It was maddening. The scent of food was everywhere. Pickles. Meat. Ketchup. Grease. Special sauce.

My fly body thought it had died and gone to heaven. Outside of a good trash dump, there's no place a fly likes more than a fast food restaurant.

<What about the Happy Meal?> Cassie asked.

<Why is the meal happy?> Ax asked.

Tobias decided to answer Cassie's question. <That's how you signal. That's the code. You go up to the counter and say, 'I'd like a Happy Meal. With extra happy.' That's the signal.>

I flew upside down along the ceiling, looking for a place to land and rest. I buzzed to a nice greasy patch near the deep fryer, turned a back flip, and set down. My mouth — actually, it was more like some insanely long straw that could curl up — extended down and began spitting digestive juices onto the grease, then sucking up the resulting goo.

Hey, I know it's gross. But it was either that or keep resisting the fly's desperate cries for food! food! food!

<After you place the Happy Meal order, you go around like you're going to the bathroom. But instead, you take the other door. The one that goes to the kitchen. You go in — and here's the cool part — you go into the walk-in refrigerator.>

<Then what?> Jake asked.

<Then I don't know. I could never see inside.>

<Okay. So here's the plan,> Jake said. <We watch till someone orders the Happy Meal with . . . what was it?>

<Extra happy,> Tobias said.

<Is it just my imagination, or did the Yeerks develop a sense of humor?> Marco asked.

<Once we have our Controller, we follow him in. No problem,> Jake said. Then he added grimly, <Oh yeah, no problem. A little picnic in the Yeerk pool. I'm sure they'll all buy that.>

<Um, Jake?> Marco said. <You said that last part out loud. We heard it.>

<Oh. Sorry.>

<Mr. Inspiration,> I said with a laugh. <Come on. Let's —>

<Uh uh uh! Don't say 'Let's do it,' Rachel!> Marco yelled.

We took turns hanging out above the counter. But we didn't have too long a wait till a woman came in and ordered a Happy Meal with "extra happy."

We buzzed easily along behind her as she went through the door and into the kitchen. Then into the walk-in refrigerator.

<Gotta get out of here, man,> I said. <This cold is slowing me down.>

<Yes, this body has no ability to regulate body temperature,> Ax observed. <What a strange idea. You humans do many unusual things.>

<Ax, I don't think we're exactly responsible for —>

<Yes, I know. I was attempting to make a joke. A human-style joke.>

<Great,> Marco muttered. <Funny Yeerks and now a funny Andalite.>

The Controller woman waited patiently and, after a few seconds, the back of the walk-in refrigerator split and opened wide.

She stepped and we flew through the opening. It really was going to be easy this time.

BrrrrEEEEET! BrrrrEEEEET! "Unauthorized life form detected." BrrrrEEEEET BrrrrEEEEET! "Unauthorized life form detected."

The Controller woman looked around. I saw her blue eyes, each the size of a swimming pool, turn and look. Through the shattered, splintered fly vision, I could see her focus.

Then she muttered under her breath, "Security fanatics. It's just a couple of lousy flies."

But the mechanical voice was giving instructions now.

"Shut your eyes tightly to protect against retinal damage from the Gleet BioFilter."

<The what?> I asked.

<Get out of here!> Ax yelled.

<What?>

<Out! Out! Out!> he yelled.

Ax never yells. So if he does yell, you have to figure it's a good idea to pay attention.

I spun around in midair the way only a fly can do, and I hauled wing for the still-open crack that led to the refrigerator.

Suddenly, the whole world blew up in a dazzling explosion of light. I felt my compound eyes melt. I flew on, blinded, blew through the rapidly narrowing crack, and hit the cold air.

<I'm blind!> I cried.

<I think we all are,> Ax said calmly. <We're lucky to be just blinded. A Gleet BioFilter destroys all life forms whose DNA is not entered into the computer controls. Andalite technology, of course. The Yeerks must have stolen the specifications.>

<Ax, are you telling me that filter thing will wipe out any life form except the one they program it for?> Jake asked.

<Yes, Prince Jake. I'm sorry to say, yes. Everything but the particular human-Controller.>

<Then we're shut off from the Yeerk pool,> Tobias said. <They must have this same technology at all the entrances now.>

It was hard to get *too* upset by the idea of being locked out of the Yeerk pool. But it was frustrating. And it kind of made me mad. I didn't like the idea of being outsmarted by the Yeerks.

<There must be some other way in,> I said.

<I'd like to know what it would be,> Marco said.

For a moment no one said anything. Then Cassie said, <Well . . . there is one way.>

<I take it back!> Marco said. <I take it back! I can tell by your tone, Cassie, I really *don't* want to know.>

The ultimate secret weapon...

ANIMORPHS

It's surprisingly simple. Amazingly affordable. And totally powerful. Unfortunately, using it means going back to the Yeerk pool. But Rachel and the other Animorphs have no choice. They have to try to slow down the invasion. If they don't, who will?

ANIMORPHS #17: THE UNDERGROUND

K.A. Applegate

COMING TO YOUR BOOKSTORE IN MARCH!

Everything is changing all over again....

‹Know The Secret›

ANIMORPHS

K. A. Applegate